More About Paddington

More About Paddington

By
MICHAEL BOND

With drawings by
Peggy Fortnum

A YEARLING BOOK

Published by
Dell Publishing
a division of
Bantam Doubleday Dell Publishing Group, Inc.
666 Fifth Avenue
New York, New York 10103

Reprinted by arrangement with
Houghton Mifflin Company

The trademark Yearling® is registered in the U.S. Patent
and Trademark Office.

Printed in the United States of America

August 1970

30 29

CONTENTS

CHAPTER ONE

A Family Group

THE BROWNS' HOUSE at number thirty-two Windsor Gardens was unusually quiet. It was a warm summer day and all the family with the exception of Paddington, who had mysteriously disappeared shortly after lunch, were sitting on the veranda enjoying the afternoon sun.

Apart from the faint rustle of paper as Mr. Brown turned the pages of an enormous book and the click of Mrs. Brown's knitting needles, the only sound came from Mrs. Bird, their housekeeper, as she prepared the tea things.

Jonathan and Judy were both much too busy piecing together a huge jig-saw puzzle to utter a word.

It was Mr. Brown who first broke the silence. " You know," he began, taking a long draw at his pipe, " it's a funny thing, but I've been through this encyclopædia a dozen times and there's no mention of a bear like Paddington."

" Ah, and there won't be," exclaimed Mrs. Bird. " Bears like Paddington are very rare. And a good thing too, if you ask me, or it would cost us a small fortune in marmalade." Mrs. Bird was always going on about Paddington's fondness for marmalade, but it was noticeable she was never without a spare jar in the larder in case of emergency.

" Anyway, Henry," said Mrs. Brown, as she put down her knitting, " why do you want to look up Paddington ?"

Mr. Brown twirled his moustache thoughtfully. " Oh, no reason in particular," he answered, vaguely. " I was interested—that's all."

Having a bear in the family was a heavy responsibility—especially a bear like Paddington—and Mr. Brown took the matter very seriously.

" The point is," he said, snapping the book shut, " if he's staying with us for good . . ."

" If ? " There was a chorus of alarm from the rest of the family, not to mention Mrs. Bird.

" What on earth do you mean, Henry ? " exclaimed Mrs. Brown. " If Paddington is staying with us for good. Of course he is."

" *As* he's staying with us," said Mr. Brown, hastily, " there are one or two things I have in mind. First of all I've been thinking of decorating the spare room for him."

There was general agreement at this. Ever since he had first arrived on the scene Paddington had occupied the guest room. Being a polite bear he had never said anything, even when he'd been turned out to make room for visitors, but it had long been thought he should have a room of his own.

" The second thing," continued Mr. Brown, " is a photograph. I think it would be nice if we could have a family group taken."

" A photograph? " exclaimed Mrs. Bird. " What a funny thing you should say that."

" Oh? " said Mr. Brown. " Why's that? "

Mrs. Bird busied herself with the teapot. " You'll see—all in good time," she said. And try as they might that was all the others could get from her.

Fortunately, she was saved any further questions, for at that moment there came a loud banging noise from the direction of the dining-room and Paddington himself appeared at the french windows. He was struggling with a large cardboard box, across the top of which lay a mysterious-looking metal object with long spikes on one end.

But it wasn't so much what he was carrying that caused a gasp of astonishment from the others. It was his general appearance.

His fur had an unusually soft, golden look about it, and his ears, or as much of them as they could see poking out from beneath the wide brim of his old hat, were as black and shiny as the tip of his nose. Even his paws and whiskers had to be seen to be believed.

Everyone sat up in amazement and Mrs. Brown dropped several stitches.

"Good heavens!" spluttered Mr. Brown, nearly spilling his tea over the encyclopædia. "What *have* you been doing to yourself?"

"I've been having a bath," said Paddington, looking most offended.

"A *bath*?" repeated Judy, slowly. "Without being asked?"

"Crikey!" said Jonathan. "We'd better put the flags out."

"You *are* all right?" asked Mr. Brown. "I mean— you're not feeling ill or anything?"

Paddington became even more injured at the excitement he had caused. It wasn't as if he *never* had a wash. In fact he had one most mornings. It was simply that he had decided views on baths in particular. Having a bath meant getting his fur wet all over and it took a long time to dry. "I only wanted to look nice for the photograph," he said, firmly.

"The photograph?" everyone echoed. It was really uncanny the way Paddington knew about things.

"Yes," said Paddington. An important expression came over his face as he bent down and started undoing the string round his cardboard box. " I've bought myself a camera."

There was a moment's silence while the Browns watched the back view of Paddington bending over the box.

" A camera," said Mrs. Brown at last. " But aren't they very expensive? "

" This one wasn't," said Paddington, breathing hard. He stood up, clutching the biggest camera the Browns had ever seen. " I bought it at a sale in the market. It was only three and sixpence! "

" Three and sixpence! " exclaimed Mr. Brown, looking most impressed. He turned to the others. " I must say I've never known a bear with such an eye for a bargain as Paddington."

" Gosh! " said Jonathan. " It's got a hood to put over your head and everything."

" What's that long thing? " asked Judy.

" That's a tripod," explained Paddington, proudly. He sat down on the floor and began unfolding the legs. " It's to stand the camera on so that it doesn't shake."

Mr. Brown picked up the camera and examined it. As he turned it over some rusty screws and several old nails fell out. " Isn't it rather old? " he asked, without thinking. " It looks as if someone's been using it as a workbox instead of a camera."

Paddington lifted the brim of his hat and gave Mr. Brown a hard stare. " It's a very rare sort," he replied. " The man in the bargain shop said so."

" Well, *I* think it's super," exclaimed Jonathan, excitedly. " Bags you take my picture first, Paddington."

" I've only got one plate," said Paddington, decidedly. " Extra ones cost a lot and I haven't any pocket money left—so I'm afraid you'll all have to be in a group."

" It certainly looks most complicated, and rather

large for a bear," remarked Mrs. Brown, as Paddington screwed the camera on to the tripod and then adjusted the legs so that they were the right height. " Are you sure you'll be able to work it ? "

" I think so," said Paddington. His voice became muffled as he disappeared underneath the black hood at the back. " Mr. Gruber lent me a book all about photography and I've been practising under the bedclothes."

Mr. Gruber, who kept an antique shop in the Portobello market, was a close friend of Paddington and
helped him with all his problems.

"Well, in that case"—Mr. Brown took charge of
the situation—"I suggest we all go on to the lawn and
let Paddington take our picture while the sun's shining."
And he led the way outside while Paddington bustled
around erecting his camera and tripod.

In a few moments Paddington announced that everything was ready and he began arranging the group as
he wanted them, running back to the camera every now
and then to peer at them through the lens.

Because the camera was so near the ground he had to
put Mr. Brown crouching in a rather uncomfortable
position behind Jonathan and Judy, with Mrs. Brown
and Mrs. Bird sitting on either side.

Although he didn't say anything, Paddington was a
bit disappointed with the view through the camera. He
could just recognise Mr. Brown because of his moustache,
but the others were much more difficult. Everyone
seemed blurred, almost as if they were standing in a
fog. It was strange, for when he took his head out of
the cloth it was quite sunny outside.

The Browns waited patiently while Paddington sat
on the grass and consulted his instruction book. Almost
at once he discovered a very interesting chapter headed
FOCUS. It explained how, if you wanted nice clear
pictures, it was important to make sure the camera was
the right distance away, and properly adjusted. It

even had a picture showing a man measuring the distance with a piece of string.

Several minutes went by, for Paddington was rather a slow reader, and there were a number of diagrams to examine.

" I hope he's not too long," said Mr. Brown. " I think I've got cramp coming on."

" He'll be disappointed if you move," said Mrs. Brown. " He took such a lot of trouble arranging us all and it really looks very nice."

" That's all very well," grumbled Mr. Brown. " You're sitting down."

" Ssh! " replied Mrs. Brown. " I think he's almost

ready now. He's doing something with a piece of string."

" What on earth is that for? " asked Mr. Brown.

" It's to measure you," said Paddington, tying a loop in the end.

" Well, if you don't mind," protested Mr. Brown, when he saw what Paddington was up to, " I'd much rather you tied the *other* end on to the camera instead of *this* end to my ear! " The rest of his sentence disappeared in a gurgle as Paddington pulled the string tight.

Paddington looked rather surprised and examined the knot round Mr. Brown's ear with interest. " I think I must have made a slip knot by mistake," he announced eventually. Paddington wasn't very good at knots—mainly because having paws made things diffi-cult for him.

" Really, Henry," said Mrs. Brown. " Don't make such a fuss. Anyone would think you'd been hurt."

Mr. Brown rubbed his ear, which had gone a funny mauve colour. " It's *my* ear," he said, " and it jolly well does hurt."

" Now where's he going? " exclaimed Mrs. Bird, as Paddington hurried off towards the house.

" I expect he's gone to measure the string," said Jonathan.

" Huh! " said Mr. Brown. " Well, I'm going to stand up."

" Henry! " said Mrs. Brown. " If you do I shall be very cross."

"It's too late anyway," groaned Mr. Brown. "My leg's gone to sleep."

Luckily for Mr. Brown, Paddington arrived back at that moment. He stared hard at the sun and then at the waiting group. "I'm afraid you'll all have to come over here," he said, after consulting his instruction book. "The sun's moved."

"I'm not surprised," grumbled Mr. Brown, as he sat on the lawn rubbing his leg. "At the rate we're going it will have set before we're finished."

"I never realised having a picture taken could be so complicated," said Mrs. Bird.

"What I'm not sure about," whispered Judy, "is why Paddington bothered having a bath if *he's* taking the photograph."

"That's a point," said Mr. Brown. "How *are* you going to be in the picture, Paddington?"

Paddington gave Mr. Brown a strange look. That was something he hadn't thought of either, but he decided to meet that difficulty when it came. He had a lot of other important things to do first. "I'm going to press the shutter," he said, after a moment's thought, "and then run round the other side."

"But even bears can't run *that* fast," persisted Mr. Brown.

"I'm sure Paddington knows best, Henry," whispered Mrs. Brown. "And even if he doesn't, for goodness sake don't say anything. If he finds out he's had a bath for nothing we shall never hear the last of it."

16

" It seems a very long hood," said Mrs. Bird, looking towards the camera. " I can't see Paddington at all."

" That's because he's small," explained Jonathan. " He's had to lower the tripod."

The Browns sat very still with a fixed smile on their faces as Paddington came out from beneath his hood.

He made some complicated adjustments to the front of the camera and then, after announcing he was about to fit the photographic plate, disappeared again.

Suddenly, to everybody's surprise, the camera and tripod began to rock backwards and forwards in a most dangerous manner.

" Good gracious! " exclaimed Mrs. Bird. " Whatever's happening now? "

" Look out! " shouted Mr. Brown. " It's coming towards us."

They all stood up and moved away, staring with wide-open eyes at the camera as it followed them. But when it got to within several feet it suddenly stopped, then turned left and headed towards a rose bush.

" I do hope he's all right," said Mrs. Brown, anxiously.

" I wonder if we ought to do anything?" said Mrs. Bird, as there was a muffled cry from Paddington.

But before anyone could reply the camera rebounded from the rose bush and shot back across the lawn. It went twice round the pond in the middle and then jumped up in the air several times before toppling over, to land with a dull thud in the middle of Mr. Brown's best flower bed.

" Good heavens! " shouted Mr. Brown, as he rushed forward. " My petunias! "

" Never mind your petunias, Henry," exclaimed Mrs. Brown. " What about Paddington? "

" Well, no wonder," said Mr. Brown as he bent down and lifted the hood. " He's got his head stuck inside the camera! "

" I should be careful, Dad," said Jonathan as Mr. Brown began pulling at Paddington's legs. " His whiskers might be caught in the shutter."

Mr. Brown stopped pulling and crawled round to peer through the lens. " I can't see anything," he said after a moment's pause. " It's all dark inside." He tapped the case and there came another faint cry from within.

" Butter! " said Mrs. Bird, hurrying towards the kitchen. " There's nothing like butter when anyone's stuck." Mrs. Bird was a great believer in butter. She had used it several times in the past when Paddington had got himself stuck.

All the same, even with Jonathan holding one end and Mr. Brown pulling on the other, it was some while before Paddington's head finally came away from the camera. He sat on the grass rubbing his ears and looking very crestfallen. Things hadn't gone at all according to plan.

" I vote," said Mr. Brown, when order had finally been restored, " that we set everything up exactly as it was before and tie a string to the shutter. Then Paddington can sit in the group with us and work it from a distance. It'll be much safer that way."

Everyone agreed that this was a good idea, and while Mr. Brown arranged the group once again, Paddington busied himself setting up his camera and fitting the photographic plate inside it—making sure to stand well back this time. There was a slight setback when he pulled the string too hard and the tripod fell over, but finally the big moment arrived. There was a click from the camera and everyone relaxed.

The man in the photographic shop looked most surprised when Mrs. Bird, all the Browns and Paddington trooped in through the door a little later.

" It's certainly a very rare sort," he said, examining Paddington's camera with interest. " Very rare. I've read about them of course—but I've never actually seen one before. It . . . it must have been kept in a pantry or something. It seems to have a lot of butter inside it."

" I had a bit of an accident when I tried to put the plate in," said Paddington.

" We're all very anxious to see the result of the photograph," added Mr. Brown, hastily. " We were wondering if you could do it for us while we wait."

The man said he would be only too pleased to oblige. From all he had seen and heard he was quite eager to see the picture, and he hurried off to his dark room leaving the Browns alone in the shop. He couldn't remember ever having a young bear photographer in the shop before.

When he returned there was a puzzled expression on

his face. " You did say you took this picture to-day? "
he asked, looking through the window at the bright
sunshine.

" That's right," said Paddington, eyeing him suspiciously.

" Well, sir "—the man held the plate up to the light
for Paddington to see—" it's nice and sharp—and I
can certainly see you all—but it looks as if it was foggy
at the time. And these patches of light—like moon-
beams—they're very odd! "

Paddington took the plate from the man and examined
it carefully. " I expect that's where I had my torch on
under the bedclothes," he said at last.

" Well, I think it's a very nice picture for a first
attempt," said Mrs. Bird. " And I'd like six postcard
prints, please. I'm sure Paddington's Aunt Lucy in Peru
would love one. She lives in the home for retired bears
in Lima," she added, for the benefit of the shopkeeper.

" Does she? " said the man, looking most impressed.
" Well, it's the first time I've ever had any pictures sent
overseas—especially to a home for retired bears in
Peru."

He thought for a moment. " I tell you what," he said,
" if I could borrow this camera for a week to put in my
shop window, I'll not only do all the prints you want
but I'll take a photograph of each of you into the bargain.
How's that? "

" I might have known," said Mr. Brown, as they
were walking home, " that if Paddington took our

photographs something odd would happen. Fancy getting all these pictures for nothing!"

"Bears always fall on their feet," said Mrs. Bird, looking at Paddington.

But Paddington wasn't listening. He was still thinking about his camera.

Early next morning he hurried down to the shop and was pleased to see it already occupied a position of honour in the middle of the window.

Underneath it was a notice which said: A VERY RARE TYPE OF EARLY CAMERA—NOW OWNED BY MR. PADDINGTON BROWN—A YOUNG LOCAL BEAR GENTLEMAN.

But Paddington was even more pleased by another notice next to it which said: AN EXAMPLE OF HIS WORK—and underneath that was his picture.

It was a little blurred and there were several paw marks near the edge, but one or two people in the neighbourhood came up and congratulated him and several of them said they could quite clearly recognise everyone in it. All in all Paddington thought it had been a very good three-and-sixpence worth.

CHAPTER TWO

A Spot of Decorating

PADDINGTON GAVE a deep sigh and pulled his hat down over his ears in an effort to keep out the noise. There was such a hullabaloo going on it was difficult to write up the notes in his scrapbook.

The excitement had all started when Mr. and Mrs. Brown and Mrs. Bird received an unexpected invitation to a wedding. Luckily both Jonathan and Judy were out for the day or things might have been far worse. Paddington hadn't been included in the invitation, but he didn't really mind. He didn't like weddings very much—apart from the free cake—and he'd been promised a piece of that whether he went or not.

All the same, he was beginning to wish everyone would hurry up and go. He had a special reason for wanting to be alone that day.

He sighed again, wiped the pen carefully on the back of his paw, and then mopped up some ink blots which somehow or other had found their way on to the table. He was only just in time, for at that moment the door burst open and Mrs. Brown rushed in.

" Ah, there you are, Paddington! " She stopped short in the middle of the room and stared at him. " Why on earth are you wearing your hat indoors? " she asked. " And why is your tongue all blue? "

Paddington stuck out his tongue as far as he could. " It *is* a funny colour," he admitted, squinting down at it with interest. " Perhaps I'm sickening for something! "

" You'll be sickening for something all right if you don't clear up this mess," grumbled Mrs. Bird as she entered. " Just look at it. Bottles of ink. Glue. Bits of paper. My best sewing scissors. Marmalade all over the table runner, and goodness knows what else."

Paddington looked around. It *was* in a bit of a state.

" I've almost finished," he announced. " I've just got to rule a few more lines and things. I've been writing my memories."

Paddington took his scrapbook very seriously and spent many long hours carefully pasting in pictures and writing up his adventures. Since he'd been at the Browns so much had happened it was now more than half full.

" Well, make sure you *do* clear everything up," said Mrs. Brown, " or we shan't bring you back any cake. Now do take care of yourself. And don't forget—when the baker comes we want two loaves." With that she waved good-bye and followed Mrs. Bird out of the room.

" You know," said Mrs. Bird, as she stepped into the car, " I have a feeling that bear has something up his paw. He seemed most anxious for us to leave."

" Oh, I don't know," said Mrs. Brown. " I don't see what he *can* do. We shan't be away all that long."

" Ah! " replied Mrs. Bird, darkly. " That's as may be. But he's been hanging about on the landing upstairs half the morning. I'm sure he's up to something."

Mr. Brown, who didn't like weddings much either, and was secretly wishing he could stay at home with Paddington, looked over his shoulder as he let in the clutch. " Perhaps I ought to stay as well," he said. " Then I could get on with decorating his new room."

" Now, Henry," said Mrs. Brown, firmly. " You're coming to the wedding and that's that. Paddington will be quite all right by himself. He's a very capable bear. And as for your wanting to get on with decorating his new room . . . you haven't done a thing towards it for over a fortnight, so I'm sure it can wait another day."

Paddington's new room had become a sore point in the Brown household. It was over two weeks since Mr.

Brown had first thought of doing it. So far he had stripped all the old wallpaper from the walls, removed the picture rails, the wood round the doors, the door handle, and everything else that was loose, or that he had made loose, and bought a lot of bright new wallpaper, some whitewash and some paint. There matters had rested.

In the back of the car Mrs. Bird pretended she hadn't heard a thing. An idea had suddenly come into her mind and she was hoping it hadn't entered Paddington's as well; but Mrs. Bird knew the workings of Paddington's mind better than most and she feared the worst. Had she but known, her fears were being realised at that very moment. Paddington was busy scratching out the words " AT A LEWSE END " in his scrapbook and was adding, in large capital letters, the ominous ones: " DECKERATING MY NEW ROOM! "

It was while he'd been writing " AT A LEWSE END " in

his scrapbook earlier in the day that the idea had come to him. Paddington had noticed in the past that he often got his best ideas when he was " at a loose end."

For a long while all his belongings had been packed away ready for the big move to his new room, and he was beginning to get impatient. Every time he wanted anything special he had to undo yards of string and brown paper.

Having underlined the words in red, Paddington cleared everything up, locked his scrapbook carefully in his suitcase, and hurried upstairs. He had several times offered to lend a paw with the decorating, but for some reason or other Mr. Brown had put his foot down on the idea and hadn't even allowed him in the room while work was in progress. Paddington couldn't quite understand why. He was sure he would be very good at it.

The room in question was an old box-room which had been out of use for a number of years, and when he entered it, Paddington found it was even more inter-esting than he had expected.

He closed the door carefully behind him and sniffed. There was an exciting smell of paint and whitewash in the air. Not only that, but there were some steps, a trestle table, several brushes, a number of rolls of wall-paper, and a big pail of whitewash.

The room had a lovely echo as well, and he spent a long time sitting in the middle of the floor while he was stirring the paint, just listening to his new voice.

There were so many different and interesting things around that it was a job to know what to do first. Eventually Paddington decided on the painting. Choosing one of Mr. Brown's best brushes, he dipped it into the pot of paint and then looked round the room for something to dab it on.

It wasn't until he had been working on the window-frame for several minutes that he began to wish he had started on something else. The brush made his arm ache, and when he tried dipping his paw in the paint pot instead and rubbing it on, more paint seemed to go on to the glass than the wooden part, so that the room became quite dark.

"Perhaps," said Paddington, waving the brush in the air and addressing the room in general, "perhaps if I do the ceiling first with the whitewash I can cover all the drips on the wall with the wallpaper."

But when Paddington started work on the whitewashing he found it was almost as hard as painting. Even by standing on tip-toe at the very top of the steps, he had a job to reach the ceiling. The bucket of whitewash was much too heavy for him to lift, so that he had to come down the steps every time in order to dip the brush in. And when he carried the brush up again, the whitewash ran down his paw and made his fur all matted.

Looking around him, Paddington began to wish he was still "at a loose end." Things were beginning to get in rather a mess again. He felt sure Mrs. Bird would have something to say when she saw it.

It was then that he had a brainwave. Paddington was a resourceful bear and he didn't like being beaten by things. Recently he had become interested in a house which was being built nearby. He had first seen it from the window of his bedroom and since then he'd spent many hours talking to the men and watching while they hoisted their tools and cement up to the top floor by means of a rope and pulley. Once, Mr. Briggs, the foreman, had even taken him up in the bucket too, and had let him lay several bricks.

Now the Browns' house was an old one and in the middle of the ceiling there was a large hook where a big lamp had once hung. Not only that, but in one corner of the room there was a thin coil of rope as well. . . .

Paddington set to work quickly. First he tied one end of the rope to the handle of the bucket. Then he climbed up the steps and passed the other end through the hook in the ceiling. But even so, when he had climbed down again, it still took him a long time to pull the bucket anywhere near the top of the steps. It was full to the brim with whitewash and very heavy, so that he had to stop every few seconds and tie the other end of the rope to the steps for safety.

It was when he undid the rope for the last time that things started to go wrong. As Paddington closed his eyes and leaned back for the final pull he suddenly felt to his surprise as if he was floating on air. It was a most strange feeling. He reached out one foot and waved it around. There was definitely nothing there. He opened one eye and then nearly let go of the rope in astonishment as he saw the bucket of whitewash going past him on its way down.

Suddenly everything seemed to happen at once. Before he could even reach out a paw or shout for help, his head hit the ceiling and there was a clang as the bucket hit the floor.

For a few seconds Paddington clung there, kicking the air and not knowing what to do. Then there was a gurgling sound from below. Looking down, he saw to

his horror that all the whitewash was running out of the bucket. He felt the rope begin to move again as the bucket got lighter, and then it shot past him again as he descended to land with a bump in the middle of a sea of whitewash.

Even then his troubles weren't over. As he tried to regain his balance on the slippery floor, he let go of the rope, and with a rushing noise the bucket shot downwards again and landed on top of his head, completely covering him.

Paddington lay on his back in the whitewash for several minutes, trying to get his breath back and wondering what had hit him. When he did sit up and take the bucket off his head he quickly put it back on again. There was whitewash all over the floor, the paint pots had been upset into little rivers of brown and green, and Mr. Brown's decorating cap was floating in one corner of the room. When Paddington saw it he felt very glad he'd left *his* hat downstairs.

One thing was certain—he was going to have a lot of explaining to do. And that was going to be even more difficult than usual, because he couldn't even explain to himself quite what had gone wrong.

It was some while later, when he was sitting on the upturned bucket thinking about things, that the idea of doing the wallpapering came to him. Paddington had a hopeful nature and he believed in looking on the bright side. If he did the wallpapering really well, the others might not even notice the mess he'd made.

Paddington was fairly confident about the wall-papering. Unknown to Mr. Brown, he had often watched him in the past through a crack in the door, and it looked quite simple. All you had to do was to brush some sticky stuff on the back of the paper and then put it on the wall. The high parts weren't too difficult, even for a bear, because you could fold the paper in two and put a broom in the middle where the fold was. Then you simply pushed the broom up and down the wall in case there were any nasty wrinkles.

Paddington felt much more cheerful now he'd thought of the wallpapering. He found some paste already mixed in another bucket, which he put on top of the trestle while he unrolled the paper. It was a little difficult at first because every time he tried to unroll the paper he had to crawl along the trestle pushing it with his paws and the other end rolled up again and followed behind him. But eventually he managed to get one piece completely covered in paste.

He climbed down off the trestle, carefully avoiding the worst of the whitewash, which by now was beginning to dry in large lumps, and lifted the sheet of wallpaper on to a broom. It was a long sheet of paper, much longer than it had seemed when he was putting the paste on, and somehow or other, as Paddington waved the broom about over his head, it began to wrap itself around him. After a struggle he managed to push his way out and headed in the general direction of a piece of wall. He stood back and surveyed the result. The

33

paper was torn in several places, and there seemed to
be a lot of paste on the outside, but Paddington felt quite
pleased with himself. He decided to try another piece,
then another, running backwards and forwards between
the trestle and the walls as fast as his legs could carry

him in an effort to get it all finished before the Browns
returned.

Some of the pieces didn't quite join, others overlapped,
and on most of them there were some very odd-looking
patches of paste and whitewash. None of the pieces
were as straight as he would have liked, but when he
put his head on one side and squinted, Paddington felt

34

the overall effect was quite nice, and he felt very pleased with himself.

It was as he was taking a final look round the room at his handiwork that he noticed something very strange. There was a window, and there was also a fireplace. But there was no longer any sign of a door. Paddington stopped squinting and his eyes grew rounder and rounder. He distinctly remembered there *had* been a door because he had come through it. He blinked at all four walls. It was difficult to see properly because the paint on the window-glass had started to dry and there was hardly any light coming through—but there most definitely wasn't a door!

" I can't understand it," said Mr. Brown as he entered the dining-room. " I've looked everywhere and there's no sign of Paddington. I told you I should have stayed at home with him."

Mrs. Brown looked worried. " Oh dear, I hope nothing's happened to him. It's so unlike him to go out without leaving a note."

" He's not in his room," said Judy.

" Mr. Gruber hasn't seen him either," added Jonathan. " I've just been down to the market and he says he hasn't seen him since they had cocoa together this morning."

" Have *you* seen Paddington anywhere? " asked Mrs. Brown as Mrs. Bird entered, carrying a tray of supper things.

" I don't know about Paddington," said Mrs. Bird.
" I've been having enough trouble over the water pipes
without missing bears. I think they've got an air lock or
something. They've been banging away ever since we
came in."

Mr. Brown listened for a moment. " It *does* sound
like water pipes," he said. " And yet . . . it isn't
regular enough, somehow." He went outside into the
hall. " It's a sort of thumping noise. . . ."

" Crikey! " shouted Jonathan. " Listen . . . it's someone sending an S.O.S."

Everyone exchanged glances and then, in one voice
cried: " Paddington! "

" Mercy me," said Mrs. Bird as they burst through
the papered-up door. " There must have been an earth-
quake or something. And either that's Paddington or
it's his ghost! " She pointed towards a small, white
figure as it rose from an upturned bucket to greet them.

" I couldn't find the door," said Paddington, plain-
tively. " I think I must have papered it over when I
did the decorating. It was there when I came in. I
remember seeing it. So I banged on the floor with a
broom handle."

" Gosh! " said Jonathan, admiringly. " What a
mess! "

" You . . . papered . . . it . . . over . . . when . . . you
. . . did . . . the . . . decorating," repeated Mr. Brown.
He was a bit slow to grasp things sometimes.

" That's right," said Paddington. " I did it as a
36

surprise." He waved a paw round the room. "I'm afraid it's in a bit of a mess, but it isn't dry yet."

While the idea was slowly sinking into Mr. Brown's mind, Mrs. Bird came to Paddington's rescue. "Now it's not a bit of good holding an inquest," she said. "What's done is done. And if you ask me it's a good thing too. Now perhaps we shall get some proper decorators in to do the job." With that she took hold of Paddington's paw and led him out of the room.

"As for you, young bear—you're going straight into a hot bath before all that plaster and stuff sets hard!"

Mr. Brown looked after the retreating figures of Mrs. Bird and Paddington and then at the long trail of white footprints and pawmarks. "Bears!" he said, bitterly.

Paddington hung about in his room for a long time after his bath and waited until the last possible minute before going downstairs to supper. He had a nasty feeling he was in disgrace. But surprisingly the word "decorating" wasn't mentioned at all that evening.

Even more surprisingly, while he was sitting up in bed drinking his cocoa, several people came to see him and each of them gave him sixpence. It was all very mysterious, but Paddington didn't like to ask why in case they changed their minds.

It was Judy who solved the problem for him when she came in to say good night.

"I expect Mummy and Mrs. Bird gave you sixpence because they don't want Daddy to do any more decorating," she explained. "He always starts things and never finishes them. And I expect Daddy gave you one because he didn't want to finish it anyway. Now they're getting a proper decorator in, so everyone's happy!"

Paddington sipped his cocoa thoughtfully. "Perhaps if I did another room I'd get another one and sixpence," he said.

"Oh, no, you don't," said Judy sternly. "You've done quite enough for one day. If I were you I shouldn't mention the word ' decorating ' for a long time to come."

"Perhaps you're right," said Paddington sleepily, as he stretched out his paws. "But I *was* at a loose end."

CHAPTER THREE

Paddington Turns Detective

THE OLD BOX-ROOM was finished at last and everyone, including Paddington, agreed that he was a very lucky bear to move into such a nice room. Not only was the paintwork a gleaming white, so that he could almost see his face in it, but the walls were gaily papered and he even had new furniture of his own as well.

"In for a penny, in for a pound!" Mr. Brown had said. And he had bought Paddington a brand new bed with special short legs, a spring mattress, and a cupboard for his odds and ends.

There were several other pieces of furniture and Mrs. Brown had been extravagant and bought a thick pile carpet for the floor. Paddington was very proud of his carpet and he'd carefully spread some old newspapers over the parts where he walked so that his paws wouldn't make it dirty.

Mrs. Bird's contribution had been some bright new curtains for the windows, which Paddington liked very much. In fact, the first night he spent in his new room he couldn't make up his mind whether to have them drawn together so that he could admire them, or left apart so that he could see the view. He got out of bed several times and eventually decided to have one drawn and the other left back so that he could have the best of both worlds.

Then something strange caught his eye. Paddington made a point of keeping a torch by the side of his bed in case there was an emergency during the night, and it was while he was flashing it on and off to admire the drawn curtain that he noticed it. Each time he flashed the torch there was an answering flicker of light from somewhere outside. He sat up in bed, rubbing his eyes, and stared in the direction of the window.

He decided to try a more complicated signal. Two short flashes followed by several long ones. When he did so he nearly fell out of bed with surprise, for each time he sent a signal it was repeated in exactly the same way through the glass.

Paddington jumped out of bed and rushed to the

window. He stayed there for a long while peering out at the garden, but he couldn't see anything at all. Having made sure the window was tightly shut, he drew both curtains and hurried back to bed, pulling the clothes over his head a little farther than usual. It was all very mysterious and Paddington didn't believe in taking any chances.

It was Mr. Brown, at breakfast the next morning, who gave him his first clue.

"Someone's stolen my prize marrow!" he announced crossly. "They must have got in during the night."

For some weeks past Mr. Brown had been carefully nursing a huge marrow which he intended to enter for a vegetable show. He watered it morning and evening and measured it every night before going to bed.

Mrs. Brown exchanged a glance with Mrs. Bird. " Never mind, Henry dear," she said. " You've got several others almost as good."

" I *do* mind," grumbled Mr. Brown. " And the others will never be as good—not in time for the show."

" Perhaps it was one of the other competitors, Dad," said Jonathan. " Perhaps they didn't want you to win. It was a jolly good marrow."

" That's quite possible," said Mr. Brown, looking more pleased at the thought. " I've a good mind to offer a small reward."

Mrs. Bird hastily poured out some more tea. Both she and Mrs. Brown appeared anxious to change the subject. But Paddington pricked up his ears at the mention of a reward. As soon as he had finished his toast and marmalade he asked to be excused and disappeared upstairs without even having a third cup of tea.

It was while she was helping Mrs. Bird with the washing-up that Mrs. Brown first noticed something odd going on in the garden.

" Look ! " she said, nearly dropping one of the breakfast plates in her astonishment. " Behind the cabbage patch. Whatever is it ? "

Mrs. Bird followed her gaze out of the window to

where something brown and shapeless kept bobbing up and down. Her face cleared. " It's Paddington," she said. " I'd recognise his hat anywhere."

" Paddington? " echoed Mrs. Brown. " But what on earth is he doing crawling about in the cabbage patch on his paws and knees? "

" He looks as if he's lost something," said Mrs. Bird. " That's Mr. Brown's magnifying glass he's got."

Mrs. Brown sighed. " Oh, well, we shall know what it is soon enough, I expect."

Unaware of the interest he was causing, Paddington sat down behind a raspberry cane and undid a small notebook which he opened at a page marked LIST OF CLEWS.

Recently Paddington had been reading a mystery story which Mr. Gruber had lent him and he had begun to fancy himself as a detective. The mysterious flashes of the night before and the loss of Mr. Brown's marrow convinced him his opportunity had come at last.

So far it had all been rather disappointing. He had found several footprints, but he'd traced them all back to the house. In the big gap left by Mr. Brown's prize marrow there were two dead beetles and an empty seed packet, but that was all.

All the same, Paddington wrote the details carefully in his notebook and drew a map of the garden—putting a large X to mark the spot where the marrow had once been. Then he went back upstairs to his room in order to think things out. When he got there he made another addition to his map—a drawing of the new house which was being built beyond the end of the garden. Paddington decided that was where the mysterious flashes must have come from the night before. He stared at it through his opera glasses for some time but the only people he could see were the builders.

Shortly afterwards, anyone watching the Browns' house would have seen the small figure of a bear emerge from the front door and make its way towards the market. Fortunately for Paddington's plans no one saw him leave, nor did anyone see him when he returned some while later carrying a large parcel in his arms. There was an excited gleam in his eyes as he crept back up the stairs and entered his bedroom, carefully locking the door behind him. Paddington liked parcels and this one was particularly interesting.

It took him a long time to undo the knots on the string because his paws were trembling with excitement, but when he did pull the paper apart it revealed a long cardboard box, very brightly coloured, with the words MASTER DETECTIVE'S DISGUISE OUTFIT on the front.

Paddington had been having a battle with himself ever since he'd first seen it several days before in a shop window. Although six shillings seemed an awful lot of money to pay for anything—especially when you only get one and sixpence a week pocket money—Paddington felt very pleased with himself as he emptied the contents on to the floor. There was a long black beard, some dark glasses, a police whistle, several bottles of chemicals marked " Handle with Care "—which Paddington hurriedly put back in the box—a fingerprint pad, a small bottle of invisible ink, and a book of instructions.

It seemed a very good disguise outfit. Paddington tried writing his name on the lid of the box with the invisible ink and he couldn't see it at all. Then he tested the fingerprint pad with his paw and blew several blasts on the police whistle under the bedclothes. He rather wished he'd thought of doing it the other way round as a lot of the ink came off on the sheets, which was going to be difficult to explain.

But he liked the beard best of all. It had two pieces of wire for fitting over the ears, and when he turned and suddenly caught sight of himself in the mirror it quite made him jump. With his hat on, and an old raincoat

45

of Jonathan's which Mrs. Brown had put out for the
jumble sale, he could hardly recognise himself. After
studying the effect in the mirror from all possible angles,
Paddington decided to try it out downstairs. It was

difficult to walk properly; Jonathan's old coat was too long for him and he kept treading on it. Apart from that, his ears didn't seem to fit the beard as well as he would have liked, so that he had to hang on to it with one paw while he went backwards down the stairs, holding on to the banisters with the other paw. He was so intent on what he was doing that he didn't hear Mrs. Bird coming up until she was right on top of him.

Mrs. Bird looked most startled when she bumped into him. " Oh, Paddington," she began, " I was just coming up to see you. I wonder if you would mind going down to the market for me and fetching half a pound of butter? "

" I'm not Paddington," said a gruff voice from behind the beard. " I'm Sherlock Holmes—the famous detective! "

" Yes, dear," said Mrs. Bird. " But don't forget the butter. We need it for lunch." With that she turned and went back down the stairs towards the kitchen. The door shut behind her and Paddington heard the murmur of voices.

He pulled off the beard disappointedly. " Thirty-six buns worth! " he said bitterly, to no one in particular. He almost felt like going back to the shop and asking for his money back. Thirty-six buns were thirty-six buns and it had taken him a long time to save that much money.

But when he got outside the front door Paddington hesitated. It seemed a pity to waste his disguise, and even if Mrs. Bird had seen through it, Mr. Briggs, the foreman at the building site, might not. Paddington decided to have one more try. He might even pick up some more clues.

By the time he arrived at the new house he was feeling

much more pleased with himself. Out of the corner of his eye he had noticed quite a number of people staring at him as he passed. And when he'd looked at them over the top of his glasses several of them had hurriedly crossed to the other side of the road.

He crept along outside the house until he heard voices. They seemed to be coming from an open window on the first floor and he distinctly recognised Mr. Briggs's voice among them. There was a ladder propped against the wall and Paddington clambered up the rungs until his head was level with the window-sill. Then he carefully peered over the edge.

Mr. Briggs and his men were busy round a small stove making themselves a cup of tea. Paddington stared hard at Mr. Briggs, who was in the act of pouring some water into the teapot, and then, after adjusting his beard, he blew a long blast on his police whistle.

There was a crash of breaking china as Mr. Briggs jumped up. He pointed a trembling hand in the direction of the window.

"Cor!" he shouted. "Look! H'an apparition!" The others followed his gaze with open mouths. Paddington stayed just long enough to see four white faces staring at him and then he slid down the ladder on all four paws and hid behind a pile of bricks. Almost immediately there was the sound of excited voices at the window.

"Can't see it now," said a voice. "Must 'ave vanished."

"Cor!" repeated Mr. Briggs, mopping his brow with a spotted handkerchief. "Whatever it was, I don't never want to see nothing like it again. Fair chilled me to the marrow it did!" With that he slammed the window shut and the voices died away.

From behind the pile of bricks Paddington could hardly believe his ears. He had never even dreamed that Mr. Briggs and his men could be mixed up in the affair. And yet—he had definitely heard Mr. Briggs say his marrow had been chilled.

After removing his beard and dark glasses, Paddington sat down behind the bricks and made several notes in his book with the invisible ink. Then he made his way slowly and thoughtfully in the direction of the grocers.

It had been a very good day's detecting, and Paddington decided he would have to pay another visit to the building site when all was quiet.

It was midnight. All the household had long since gone to bed.

"You know," said Mrs. Brown, just as the clock was striking twelve, "it's a funny thing, but I'm sure Paddington's up to something."

"There's nothing funny in that," replied Mr. Brown, sleepily. "He's always up to *something*. What is it this time?"

"That's just the trouble," said Mrs. Brown. "I don't really know. But he was wandering around wearing a false beard this morning. He nearly startled poor Mrs. Bird out of her wits. He's been writing things in his notebook all the evening too, and do you know what?"

"No," said Mr. Brown, stifling a yawn. "What?"

"When I looked over his shoulder there was nothing there!"

"Oh well, bears will be bears," said Mr. Brown. He paused for a moment as he reached up to turn out the light. "That's strange," he said. "I could have sworn I heard a police whistle just then."

"Nonsense, Henry," said Mrs. Brown. "You must be dreaming."

Mr. Brown shrugged his shoulders as he turned out the light. He was much too tired to argue. All the same he knew he *had* heard a whistle. But as he closed his eyes and prepared himself for sleep, it never crossed his mind that the cause of it might be Paddington.

Lots of things had been happening to Paddington since he'd crept out of the Browns' house under cover of darkness and made his way round to the building site. So many things had happened, one after the other, that he almost wished he'd never decided to be a detective in the first place. He felt very glad when, in answer to several loud blasts on his whistle, a large black car drew up at the side of the road and two men in uniform got out.

"Hallo, hallo," said the first of the men, looking hard at Paddington. "What's going on here?"

Paddington pointed a paw dramatically in the direction of the new house. "I've captured a burglar!" he announced.

"A *what*?" asked the second policeman, peering at Paddington. He'd come across some very strange things in the course of duty, but he'd never been called out in the middle of the night by a young bear before.

This one seemed to be wearing a long black beard and a duffle coat. It was most unusual.

"A burglar," repeated Paddington. "I think he's the one that took Mr. Brown's marrow!"

"Mr. Brown's marrow?" repeated the first police-

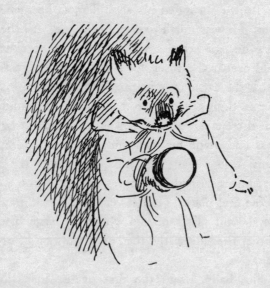

man, looking rather dazed as he followed Paddington through his secret entrance into the house.

"That's right," said Paddington. "Now he's got my marmalade sandwiches. I took a big parcel of them inside with me in case I got hungry while I was waiting."

"Of course," said the second policeman, trying to

humour Paddington. " Marmalade sandwiches." He tapped his forehead as he looked at his colleague. " And where is the burglar now—eating your sandwiches?"

" I expect so," said Paddington. " I shut him in the room and I put a piece of wood under the door so that he couldn't get out. I got my beard caught in one of the sandwiches—so I switched my torch on to take some of the hairs out of the marmalade and then it happened!"

" *What* happened?" chorused the policemen. They were finding it rather difficult to keep up with Paddington's description of the course of events.

" I saw someone flashing a light outside the window," explained Paddington, as patiently as he could. " Then I heard footsteps coming up the stairs, so I lay in wait." He pointed towards a door at the top of the stairs. " He's in there!"

Before either of the policemen could ask any more questions there came the sound of banging and a voice cried, " Let me out!"

" Good heavens!" exclaimed the first policeman. " There *is* someone in there!" He looked at Paddington with renewed respect. " Did you get a description, sir?"

" He was about eight feet tall," said Paddington, recklessly, " and he sounded very cross when he found he couldn't get out."

" Hmm!" said the second policeman. " Well, we'll soon see about that. Stand back!" With that he pulled the piece of wood from under the door and flung it open, shining his torch into the room.

Everyone stood back and waited for the worst to happen. To their surprise, when the man came out it was another policeman.

" Locked in ! " he exclaimed, bitterly. " I see some lights flashing from an empty house, so I go to investigate . . . and what happens ? I'm locked in . . . by a *bear* ! " He pointed towards Paddington. " And if I'm not mistaken, that's him ! "

Paddington suddenly began to feel very small. All three policemen were looking at him, and in the excitement his beard had fallen off one ear.

" Hmm," said the first policeman. " And what were *you* doing in an empty house at gone midnight, young fellow me bear? And wearing a disguise at that! I can see we shall have to take you along to the station for questioning."

" It's a bit difficult to explain," said Paddington, sadly. " I'm afraid it's going to take rather a long time. You see . . . it's all to do with Mr. Brown's marrow— the one he was going to enter for the vegetable show . . ."

The policemen weren't the only ones who found it all rather hard to understand. Mr. Brown was still asking questions long after Paddington had been returned from the police station to their safe keeping.

" I still don't see how my losing a marrow has got anything to do with Paddington being arrested," he said for the hundredth time.

" But Paddington wasn't arrested, Henry," said Mrs. Brown. " He was only detained for questioning. Anyway, he was only trying to get your marrow back for you. You ought to be very grateful."

She sighed. She would have to tell her husband the truth sooner or later. She'd already told Paddington. " I'm afraid it's all my fault really," she said. " You see . . . *I* cut your marrow by mistake! "

" *You* did? " exclaimed Mr. Brown. " You cut my prize marrow? "

" Well, I didn't realise it was your prize one," said Mrs. Brown. " And you know how fond you are of stuffed marrow. We had it for dinner last night! "

Back in his own room, Paddington felt quite pleased with himself as he got into bed. He'd have a lot to tell his friend, Mr. Gruber, in the morning. Once the inspector at the police station had heard his full story he had complimented Paddington on his bravery and ordered his immediate release.

" I wish there were more bears about like you, Mr. Brown," he had said. And he had given Paddington a real police whistle as a souvenir. Even the policeman who had been locked in said he quite understood how it had all come about.

Besides, he had solved the mystery of the flashing lights at last. It hadn't been anyone in the garden at all, but simply the reflection of his own torch on the window. When he stood up on the end of the bed he could even see himself quite plainly in the glass.

In a way Paddington was sorry about the marrow. Especially as he wouldn't get the reward. But he was very glad the culprit hadn't been Mr. Briggs. He liked Mr. Briggs—and besides, he'd been promised another ride in his bucket. He didn't want to miss that.

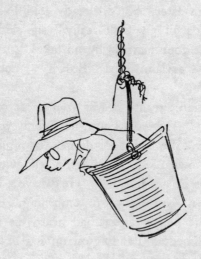

CHAPTER FOUR

Paddington and the Bonfire

SOON AFTER the marrow adventure the weather changed.
It began to get colder. The leaves fell from the trees
and it became dark very early in the evenings. Jonathan
and Judy went back to school and Paddington was left
on his own for much of the day.

But one morning, towards the end of October, a letter
arrived with his name on the envelope. It was marked
" Urgent " and " Strictly Personal " and it was in
Jonathan's writing. Paddington didn't get many letters,

only an occasional picture postcard from his Aunt Lucy in Peru, so it was all the more exciting.

In some ways it was a rather mysterious letter and Paddington couldn't make head or tail of it. In it Jonathan asked him to collect all the dry leaves he could find and sweep them into a pile ready for when he came home in a few days' time. Paddington puzzled about it for a long time, and in the end he decided to consult his friend Mr. Gruber on the subject. Mr. Gruber knew about most things, and even if he couldn't tell the answer to a question straight away, he had a huge library of books in his antique shop and knew just where to look. He and Paddington often had a long chat about things in general over their morning cocoa, and Mr. Gruber liked nothing better than to help Paddington with his problems.

" A problem shared is a problem halved, Mr. Brown," he was fond of saying. " And I must say, that since you came to live in the district I've never been short of things to look up."

As soon as he had finished his breakfast, Paddington put on his scarf and duffle coat, collected the morning shopping list from Mrs. Bird, and set off with his basket on wheels towards the shops in the Portobello Road.

Paddington enjoyed shopping. He was a popular bear with the street traders in the market, even though he usually struck a hard bargain. He always compared the prices on the various stalls very carefully before actually buying anything. Mrs. Bird said he made the housekeeping money go twice as far as anyone else.

It was even colder outside than Paddington had expected, and when he stopped to look in a newsagent's on the way, his breath made the bottom of the window quite cloudy. Paddington was a polite bear, and when he saw the shopkeeper glaring at him through the door he carefully rubbed the steamy part with his paw in case anyone else wanted to look in. As he did so he suddenly noticed that the inside of the window had changed since he'd last passed that way.

Before, it had been full of chocolate and sweets. Now they were all gone and in their place was a very ragged-looking dummy sitting on top of a pile of logs. It held a notice in its hand which said:

REMEMBER, REMEMBER, THE FIFTH OF NOVEMBER, GUNPOWDER, TREASON AND PLOT.

And underneath that was an even larger notice saying:

GET YOUR FIREWORKS HERE!

Paddington studied it all carefully for a few moments and then hurried on to Mr. Gruber's, pausing only to pick up his morning supply of buns at the bakery, where he had a standing order.

Now that the cold weather had set in, Mr. Gruber no longer sat on the pavement in front of his shop in the morning. Instead, he had arranged a sofa by the stove in the back of the shop. It was a cosy corner,

surrounded by books, but Paddington didn't like it quite
so much as being outside. For one thing, the sofa was
an old one and some of the horsehairs poked through,
but he quickly forgot about this as he handed Mr.
Gruber his share of buns and began telling him of the
morning's happenings.

"Gunpowder, treason and plot?" said Mr. Gruber,
as he handed Paddington a large mug of steaming cocoa.
"Why, that's to do with Guy Fawkes' day."

He smiled apologetically and rubbed the steam from
his glasses when he saw that Paddington still looked
puzzled.

"I always forget, Mr. Brown," he said, "that you

come from Darkest Peru. I don't suppose you know about Guy Fawkes."

Paddington wiped the cocoa from his whiskers with the back of his paw in case it left a stain and shook his head.

"Well," continued Mr. Gruber. "I expect you've seen fireworks before. I seem to remember when I was in South America many years ago they always had them on fête days."

Paddington nodded. Now that Mr. Gruber mentioned it, he did remember his Aunt Lucy taking him to a firework display. Although he'd only been very small at the time he had enjoyed it very much.

"We only have fireworks once a year here," said Mr. Gruber. "On November the Fifth." And then he went on to tell Paddington all about the plot to blow up the Houses of Parliament many years ago, and how its discovery at the last moment had been celebrated ever since by the burning of bonfires and letting off of fireworks.

Mr. Gruber was very good at explaining things and Paddington thanked him when he had finished.

Mr. Gruber sighed and a far away look came into his eyes. "It's a long time since I had any fireworks of my own, Mr. Brown," he said. "A very long time indeed."

"Well, Mr. Gruber," said Paddington, importantly. "I think we're going to have a display. You must come to ours."

Mr. Gruber looked so pleased at being invited that Paddington hurried off at once to finish his shopping. He was anxious to get back to the newsagent's quickly so that he could investigate the fireworks properly.

When he entered the shop the man looked at him doubtfully over the top of the counter. " Fireworks? " he said. " I'm not sure that I'm supposed to serve young bears with fireworks."

Paddington gave him a hard stare. " In Darkest Peru," he said, remembering all that Mr. Gruber had told him, "we had fireworks every fête day."

" I dare say," said the man. " But this isn't Darkest Peru—nor nothing like it. What do you want—bangers or the other sort? "

" I think I'd like to try some you can hold in the paw for a start," said Paddington.

The man hesitated. " All right," he said. " I'll let you have a packet of best sparklers. But if you singe your whiskers don't come running to me grumbling and wanting your money back."

Paddington promised he would be very careful and was soon hurrying back up the road towards the Browns' house. As he rounded the last corner he bumped into a small boy wheeling a pram.

The boy held out a cap containing several coppers and touched his hat respectfully. " Penny for the Guy, sir."

" Thank you very much," said Paddington, taking a penny out of the cap. " It's very kind of you."

"Oi!" said the boy as Paddington turned to go.
"Oi! You're supposed to give *me* a penny—not take
one yourself."

Paddington stared at him. "Give *you* a penny?"
he said, hardly able to believe his ears. "What for?"

"For the Guy, of course," said the boy. "That's
what I said—a penny for the Guy!" He pointed to the
pram and Paddington noticed for the first time that there
was a figure inside it. It was dressed in an old suit and
wearing a mask. It looked just like the one he'd seen
in the shop window earlier that morning.

Paddington was so surprised that he had undone his
suitcase and placed a penny in the boy's hat before he
really knew what he was doing.

"If you don't like giving a penny for the Guy," said
the small boy as he turned to go, "why don't you get

one of your own? All you need is an old suit and a bit of straw."

Paddington was very thoughtful as he made his way home. He even almost forgot to ask for a second helping at lunch.

" I do hope he hasn't hit on another of his ideas," said Mrs. Brown, as Paddington asked to be excused and disappeared into the garden. " It's most unlike him to have to be reminded about things like that. Especially when it's stew. He's usually so fond of dumplings."

" I expect it is an Idea," said Mrs. Bird, ominously. " I know the signs."

" Well, I expect the fresh air will do him good," said Mrs. Brown, looking out of the window. " And it's very good of him to offer to sweep up all the leaves. The garden's in such a mess."

" It's November," said Mrs. Bird. "Guy Fawkes!"

" Oh! " said Mrs. Brown. " *Oh dear*! "

For the next hour Paddington enjoyed himself in the garden with Mrs. Bird's dustpan and brush. The Browns had a number of trees and very soon he had a large pile of leaves, almost twice his own height, in the middle of the cabbage patch. It was while he was sitting down for a rest in the middle of a flower bed that he felt someone watching him.

He looked up to see Mr. Curry, the Browns' next door neighbour, eyeing him suspiciously over the fence. Mr. Curry wasn't very fond of bears and he was always trying to catch Paddington doing something he shouldn't so that he could report him. He had a reputation in the neighbourhood for being mean and disagreeable, and the Browns had as little to do with him as possible.

" What are you doing, bear? " he growled at Paddington. " I hope you're not thinking of setting light to all those leaves."

" Oh, no," said Paddington. " It's for Guy Fawkes."

" Fireworks! " said Mr. Curry, grumpily. " Nasty things. Banging away and frightening people."

Paddington, who had been toying with the idea of trying out one of his sparklers, hastily hid the packet behind his back. " Aren't you having any fireworks then, Mr. Curry? " he asked, politely.

" Fireworks? " Mr. Curry looked at Paddington with distaste. " Me? I can't afford them, bear. Waste of money. And what's more, if I get any coming over in *my* garden I shall report the whole matter to the police! "

Paddington felt very glad he hadn't tested his sparkler.

" Mind you, bear "—a sly gleam came into Mr. Curry's eye and he looked round carefully to make sure no one else was listening—" if anyone likes to invite me to their firework display, that's a different matter." He signalled Paddington over to the fence and began whispering in his ear. As Paddington listened his face got longer and longer and his whiskers began to sag.

" I think it's disgraceful," said Mrs. Bird later on that day when she heard that Mr. Curry had invited himself to the firework party. "Frightening a young bear like that with talk of police and such like. Just because he's too mean to buy his own fireworks. It's a good job he didn't say it to me—I'd have told him a thing or two!"

"Poor Paddington," said Mrs. Brown. "He looked most upset. Where is he now?"

"I don't know," said Mrs. Bird. "He's gone off somewhere looking for some straw. I expect it's to do with his bonfire."

She returned to the subject of Mr. Curry. "When I think of all the errands that young bear's run for him—wearing his paws to the bone—just because he's too lazy to go himself."

"He does take advantage of people," said Mrs. Brown. "Why, he even left his old suit on the porch this morning to be collected by our laundry for cleaning."

"Did he?" exclaimed Mrs. Bird, grimly. "Well, we'll soon see about *that*!" She hurried out to the front door and then called out to Mrs. Brown. "You *did* say the porch?"

"That's right," replied Mrs. Brown. "In the corner."

"It's not there now," called Mrs. Bird. "Someone must have taken it away."

"That's very strange," said Mrs. Brown. "I didn't hear anyone knock. And the laundryman hasn't been yet. How very odd."

"It'll serve him right," said Mrs. Bird, as she

returned to the kitchen, "if someone's taken it. That'll teach him a lesson!" In spite of her stern appearance, Mrs. Bird was a kindly soul at heart, but she became very cross when people took advantage of others, especially Paddington.

"Oh well," said Mrs. Brown. "I expect it'll sort itself out. I must try and remember to ask Paddington if he's seen it when he comes in."

As it happened Paddington was gone for quite a long time, so that when he did finally return, Mrs. Brown had forgotten all about the matter. It had been dark for some time when he let himself into the garden by the back way. He pushed his basket up the path until he reached Mr. Brown's shed, and then, after a struggle, managed to lift a large object out of the basket, and place it in a corner behind the lawn-mower. There was also a small cardboard box marked GI FAWKS, which rattled when he shook it.

Paddington shut the door of the shed, carefully hid the cardboard box underneath his hat in the bottom of the basket, and then crept quietly out of the garden and round to the front door. He felt pleased with himself. It had been a very good evening's work indeed—much better than he had expected—and that night, before he went to sleep, he spent a long time writing a letter to Jonathan in which he told him all about it.

"Gosh, Paddington," exclaimed Jonathan, several days later, when they were getting ready for the display.

67

"What a super lot of fireworks!" He peered into the cardboard box, which was full almost to the brim. "I've never seen so many."

"Honestly, Paddington," said Judy, admiringly. "Anyone would think you'd been collecting in the street or something."

Paddington waved a paw vaguely through the air and exchanged a knowing glance with Jonathan. But before he had time to explain things to Judy, Mr. Brown entered the room.

He was dressed in an overcoat and gumboots and he was carrying a lighted candle. "Right," he said. "Are we all ready? Mr. Gruber's waiting in the hall and Mrs. Bird's got the chairs all ready on the veranda." Mr. Brown looked as eager as anyone to start the firework display and he eyed Paddington's box enviously.

"I vote," he said, holding up his hand for silence when they were all outside in the garden, "that as this is Paddington's first November the Fifth, we let him set off the first firework."

"Hear! Hear!" applauded Mr. Gruber. "What sort would you like, Mr. Brown?"

Paddington looked thoughtfully at the box. There were so many different shapes and sizes it was difficult to decide.

" I think I'll have one of those you can hold in the paw first," he said. " I think I'll have a sparkler."

" Dull things, sparklers," said Mr. Curry, who was sitting in the best chair helping himself to some marmalade sandwiches.

" If Paddington wants a sparkler, he shall have one," said Mrs. Bird, giving Mr. Curry a freezing look.

Mr. Brown handed Paddington the candle, taking care not to let the hot fat drip on to his fur, and there was a round of applause as the sparkler burst into life. Paddington waved it over his head several times and there was another round of applause as he moved it up and down to spell out the letters P-A-D-I-N-G-T-U-N.

" Very effective," said Mr. Gruber.

" But that's not how you spell *Paddington*," grumbled Mr. Curry, his mouth full of sandwich.

" It's how *I* spell it," said Paddington. He gave Mr. Curry one of his special hard stares, but unfortunately it was dark and so the full effect was lost.

" How about lighting the bonfire? " said Mr. Brown hurriedly. " Then we can all see what we're doing." There was a crackle from the dried leaves as he bent down to apply the match.

" That's better," said Mr. Curry, rubbing his hands together. " I find it rather draughty on this veranda of yours. I think I'll let off a few more fireworks if there are no more sandwiches left." He looked across at Mrs. Bird.

" There aren't," said Mrs. Bird. " You've just had

the last one. Honestly," she continued, as Mr. Curry moved away and began rummaging in Paddington's box. " The cheek of some people. And he never even brought so much as a Catherine Wheel himself."

" He does spoil things," said Mrs. Brown. " Everyone's been looking forward to this evening. I've a good mind . . ." Whatever Mrs. Brown had been about to say was lost as there came a cry from the direction of the garden shed.

" Crikey, Paddington," shouted Jonathan. " Why ever didn't you tell us? "

" Tell us what? " asked Mr. Brown, trying to divide his attention between a Roman Candle which had just fizzled out and the mysterious object which Jonathan was dragging from the shed.

" It's a Guy! " shouted Judy with delight.

" It's a super one too! " exclaimed Jonathan. " It looks just like a real person. Is it yours, Paddington? "

" Well," said Paddington, " yes . . . and no." He looked rather worried. In the excitement he had quite forgotten about the Guy which he'd used when he'd collected the money for the fireworks. He wasn't at all sure he wanted the others to know about it in case too many questions were asked.

" A Guy? " said Mr. Curry. " Then it had better go on the bonfire." He peered at it through the smoke. For some odd reason there was a familiar look about it which he couldn't quite place.

" Oh, no," said Paddington, hurriedly. " I don't

think you'd better do that. It's not really for burning."

"Nonsense, bear," said Mr. Curry. "I can see you don't know much about Guy Fawkes' night. Guys are always burned." He pushed the others on one side and with the help of Mr. Brown's garden rake placed the Guy on top of the bonfire.

"There!" he exclaimed, as he stood back rubbing his hands. "That's better. That's what I call a bonfire."

Mr. Brown removed his glasses, polished them, and then looked hard at the bonfire. He didn't recognise the suit the Guy was wearing and he was glad to see it wasn't one of his. All the same, he had a nasty feeling at the back of his mind. "It . . . it seems a very well dressed sort of Guy," he remarked.

Mr. Curry started and then stepped forward to take a closer look. Now that the bonfire was well and truly alight it was easier to see. The trousers were blazing merrily and the jacket had just started to smoulder. His eyes nearly popped out and he pointed a trembling finger towards the flames.

"That's my suit!" he roared. "My suit! The one you were supposed to send to the cleaners!"

"What!" exclaimed Mr. Brown. Everyone turned to look at Paddington.

Paddington was as surprised as the others. It was the first he had heard of Mr. Curry's suit. "I found it on the doorstep," he said. "I thought it had been put out for the rummage sale. . . ."

"The *rummage sale*?" cried Mr. Curry, almost

beside himself with rage. " The *rummage sale*? My best suit! I'll . . .I'll . . ." Mr. Curry was spluttering so much he couldn't think of anything to say. But Mrs. Bird could.

" To start with," she said, " it wasn't your best suit. It's been sent to the cleaners at least six times to my knowledge. And I'm quite sure Paddington didn't know it was yours. In any case," she finished triumphantly, " who was it insisted it should go on the bonfire in the first place? "

Mr. Brown tried hard not to laugh, and then he caught Mr. Gruber's eye looking at him over the top of his handkerchief. " You *did*, you know," he spluttered. " You said put it on the bonfire. And Paddington tried to stop you! "

Mr. Curry struggled hard for a moment as he looked from one to the other. But he knew when he was beaten. He gave one final glare all round the party and then slammed the door behind him.

" Well," chuckled Mr. Gruber, " I must say that when young Mr. Brown's around there's never a dull moment! " He felt underneath his chair and brought out a cardboard box. " Now I vote we get on with the display. And just in case we run out of fireworks—I've brought a few more along."

" You know, it's funny you should say that," said Mr. Brown, feeling under *his* chair. " But I have some as well! "

Afterwards everyone in the neighbourhood voted it

was the best firework display they had seen for many a year. Quite a number of people turned up to watch, and even Mr. Curry was seen peeping from behind his curtains on several occasions.

And as Paddington lifted a tired paw and waved the last sparkler in the air to spell out the words T-H-E E-N-D, everyone agreed they had never seen such a successful bonfire before—or such a well-dressed Guy.

CHAPTER FIVE

Trouble at Number Thirty-two

THAT EVENING, after the bonfire had died away, the
weather suddenly became even colder. When Paddington went upstairs to bed he opened his window a few
inches and peeped out in case there were any more fireworks to see. He sniffed the cold night air and then
hastily shut the window, diving into bed and pulling
the blankets over his ears.

In the morning he woke much earlier than usual,
shivering with the cold, and found to his surprise that
the ends of his whiskers, which had become uncovered

during the night, were quite stiff. Having listened for
a while to make sure breakfast was being cooked, he put
on his duffle coat and went along to the bathroom.

When he reached the bathroom, Paddington made
several interesting discoveries. First, his flannel, which
he'd left folded over the towel rail the night before, was
as stiff as a board, and it made a funny cracking noise
when he tried to bend it straight. Then, when he turned
the tap, nothing happened. Paddington decided quite
quickly that he wasn't meant to wash that morning and
hurried back to his own room.

But when he got there he had yet another surprise.
He drew the curtains and tried to look out of his window,
only to find that it was all white and frosted—just like
the one in the bathroom. Paddington breathed heavily
on the glass and rubbed it with the back of his paw.
When he had made a hole big enough to peer through,
he nearly fell over backwards with astonishment.

All traces of the previous evening's bonfire had
completely vanished. Instead, everything was covered
by a thick blanket of white. Not only that, but there were
millions of large white flakes falling out of the sky.

He rushed downstairs to tell the others. The Browns
were all sitting round the breakfast table when he burst
into the dining-room. Paddington waved his paws
wildly in the air and called for them to look out of the
window.

" Good heavens! " exclaimed Mr. Brown, looking
up from his morning paper. " What *is* the matter? "

" Look! " said Paddington, pointing towards the garden. " Everything's gone white! "

Judy threw back her head and laughed. " It's all right, Paddington—it's only snow. It happens every year."

" Snow? " said Paddington, looking puzzled. "What's snow? "

" It's a nuisance," said Mr. Brown, crossly. Mr. Brown wasn't in a very good mood that morning. He hadn't expected the weather to change so quickly and all the upstairs water pipes had frozen. To make matters worse, everyone had been blaming him because he'd forgotten to stoke the boiler before going to bed.

" Snow? " said Judy. " Well, it's . . it's sort of frozen rain. It's very soft."

" Jolly good for snowballs," exclaimed Jonathan. " We'll show you how to make them after breakfast. We can clear the paths at the same time."

Paddington sat down at the breakfast table and began undoing his napkin, hardly able to take his eyes off the scene outside the window.

" Paddington! " said Mrs. Brown, suspiciously " Did you wear your duffle coat when you washed this morning? "

" A lick and a promise," said Mrs. Bird, as she handed him a steaming bowl of porridge. " And more promise than lick if you ask me."

But Paddington was much too busy thinking about the snow to hear what they were saying. He was wondering if he could speed up the breakfast by having all his things on the one plate. But just as he reached out for the bacon and eggs and the marmalade, he caught Mrs. Bird's eye and hurriedly pretended he was only conducting to the music on the wireless.

" If you do go out after breakfast, Paddington," said Mrs. Brown, " I think it would be nice if you could clear Mr. Curry's path for him before you do ours. We all know it wasn't your fault about his suit last night, but it would show you mean well."

" That's a good idea," exclaimed Jonathan. " We'll give you a hand. Then we can use all the snow we get to build a snowman this afternoon. How about it, Paddington ? "

Paddington looked rather doubtful. Whenever he tried to do anything for Mr. Curry, something always seemed to go wrong.

" But no playing snowballs," warned Mrs. Bird. " Mr. Curry always sleeps with his bedroom window open—even in the middle of winter. If you wake him he won't like it at all."

Paddington, Jonathan and Judy agreed to be as quiet as they could and as soon as breakfast was over they dressed in their warmest clothes and rushed outside to look at the snow.

Paddington was very impressed. It was much deeper than he had expected, but not at all as cold as he thought it would be, except when he stood for very long in the one place. Within a few minutes all three were busy

with shovels and brooms clearing Mr. Curry's paths for him.

Jonathan and Judy started on the pavement outside the house. Paddington fetched his seaside bucket and spade and began work on Mr. Curry's back garden path, which was not quite so wide.

He filled his bucket with snow and then tipped it through a hole in the Browns' fence near the place they intended building a snowman later in the day. It was hard work, for the snow was deep and came right up to the edge of his duffle coat, and as fast as he cleared a space, more snow came down, covering the part he'd just done.

After working for what seemed like hours, Paddington decided to have a rest. But no sooner had he settled himself on the bucket than something hit him on the back of the head, nearly knocking his hat off into the bargain.

" Caught you! " yelled Jonathan with delight. " Come on, Paddington—make yourself some snowballs—then we can have a fight."

Paddington jumped up from his bucket and dodged round the side of Mr. Curry's shed. Then, after first making sure Mrs. Bird was nowhere in sight, he gathered up some snow and rolled it into a hard ball. Holding it firmly in his right paw he closed his eyes and took careful aim.

" Yah! " shouted Jonathan, as Paddington opened his eyes. " Missed me by a mile. You'd better get some practise in! "

Paddington stood behind Mr. Curry's shed scratching his head and examining his paw. He knew the snowball must have gone somewhere but he hadn't the least idea where. After thinking about it for some time he decided to have another go. If he crept very quietly round the side of the house he might even be able to catch Jonathan unawares and get his own back.

It was as he tip-toed past Mr. Curry's back door, clutching a snowball in his paw, that he noticed for the first time the door was open. The wind was blowing the snow through into the kitchen and there was already a small pile of it on the mat. Paddington hesitated for a moment and then pulled the door shut. There was a click as it closed, and he carefully tested it with his paw to make certain it was properly fastened. He was sure Mr. Curry wouldn't want snow all over his kitchen floor, and he felt very pleased at being able to do another good deed—apart from sweeping the path.

To Paddington's surprise, when he peered round the corner at the front of the house Mr. Curry was already there. He was wearing a dressing gown over his pyjamas and he looked cold and cross. He broke off his conversation with Jonathan and Judy and stared in Paddington's direction.

" Ah, there you are, bear! " he exclaimed. " Have you been throwing snowballs? "

" Snowballs? " repeated Paddington, hurriedly putting his paw behind his back. " Did you say snowballs, Mr. Curry? "

"Yes," said Mr. Curry. "*Snowballs*! A large one came through my bedroom window a moment ago and landed right in the middle of my bed. Now it's all melted on my hot-water bottle! If I thought you had done it on purpose, bear . . ."

"Oh no, Mr. Curry," said Paddington, earnestly. "I wouldn't do a thing like that *on purpose*. I don't think I could. It's difficult throwing snowballs by paw—especially big ones like that."

"Like what?" asked Mr. Curry, suspiciously.

"Like the one you said landed in your bed," said

Paddington, sounding rather confused. He was beginning to wish Mr. Curry would hurry up and go. The
snowball was making his paw very cold.

" Mmm," said Mr. Curry. " Well I'm not standing
out here in the snow discussing bears' pranks. I came
downstairs intending to tell you off." He looked round
approvingly at the clean pavement. " But I must admit
I've been pleasantly surprised. In fact," he turned to
go back indoors, " if you make as good a job of the rest
I might even give you a penny! "

" Between you," he added, in case they mistook his
meaning.

" A penny! " exclaimed Jonathan, disgustedly. " One
measly penny."

" Oh, well," said Judy, " at least we've done our good
deed for the day. It should last for a while—even with
Mr. Curry."

Paddington looked doubtful. " I don't think it'll
last *very* long," he said, listening hard. " In fact, I
think it's nearly over." Even as he spoke there came a
roar of rage from Mr. Curry followed by several loud
bangs.

" Whatever's up now? " exclaimed Judy. " That
sounds like Mr. Curry banging on his back door."

" I thought I was doing him a good turn," said
Paddington, looking very worried, " so I shut it. I
think he must be locked out."

" Oh gosh, Paddington," groaned Judy. " You are
an unlucky bear to-day."

"Who shut my door?" roared Mr. Curry, as he strode round to the front again. "Who locked me out of my house? Bear!" he barked. "Where are you, bear?"

Mr. Curry glared down the road but there was not a soul in sight. If he had been a little less cross, he might have noticed three distinct sets of paw- and footprints where Paddington, Jonathan and Judy had beaten a hasty retreat.

After a distance the three tracks separated. Jonathan's and Judy's disappeared into the Browns' house. Paddington's went towards the market.

He had seen quite enough of Mr. Curry for one day. Besides, it had gone half-past ten and he had promised to meet Mr. Gruber for morning cocoa at eleven.

"I really think Mr. Curry has gone a bit funny in the head," said Mrs. Brown, later that day. "He was standing outside the house in his pyjamas and dressing gown this morning—in all that snow. Then he started running around in circles waving his fist."

"Mmm," replied Mrs. Bird. "I saw Paddington playing snowballs in his back garden just before that happened."

"Oh dear," said Mrs. Brown. She looked out of the window. The sky had cleared at last and the garden, with all the trees bowed down under the weight of snow, looked just like a Christmas card. "It seems very still," she said. "Almost as if something was about to happen."

Mrs. Bird followed her gaze. "They've made a wonderful snowman. I've never seen quite such a good one before. It's only small but it looks most lifelike."

"Isn't that Paddington's old hat they've put on top?" asked Mrs. Brown. She looked round as the door opened and Jonathan and Judy entered the room. "We were just saying," she continued. "What a lovely snowman you've made."

"It isn't a snowman," said Jonathan, mysteriously. "It's a snow*bear*. It's meant to be a surprise for Dad. He's coming down the road now."

"It looks as if he'll have more than one surprise coming his way," said Mrs. Bird. "I can see Mr. Curry waiting for him by the fence."

"Oh, crikey!" groaned Jonathan. "That's torn it."

"Trust Mr. Curry to spoil things," said Judy. "I hope he doesn't keep Dad talking too long."

"Why, dear?" asked Mrs. Brown. "Does it matter?"

"Does it *matter*?" cried Jonathan, rushing to the window. "I'll say it does!"

Mrs. Brown didn't pursue the subject. She had no doubt that she would hear all about it in due course— whatever it was.

It took Mr. Brown a long time to get rid of Mr. Curry and put his car away in the garage. When he did come indoors he looked very fed up.

"That Mr. Curry," he exclaimed. "Telling tales about Paddington again. If I'd been there this morning he'd have got more than a snowball in his bed." He looked round the room. " By the way, where *is* Paddington?" Paddington usually liked helping Mr. Brown put his car away and it was most unusual for him not to be there ready to give paw signals.

" I haven't seen him for ages," said Mrs. Brown. She looked at Jonathan and Judy. " Do *you* know where he is?"

" Didn't he jump out at you, Dad?" asked Jonathan.

" Jump out at me?" exclaimed Mr. Brown, looking puzzled. " Not that I know of. Why, was he supposed to?"

" But you saw the snowbear, didn't you?" asked Judy. " Just by the garage."

" Snow*bear*?" said Mr. Brown. " Good heavens— you don't mean—that wasn't Paddington?"

" What's that young bear been up to now?" asked Mrs. Bird. " Do you mean to say he's been out there covered in snow all this time? I've never heard of such a thing."

" Well, it wasn't really his idea," said Jonathan. " Not all of it."

" I expect he heard Mr. Curry's voice and got frightened," said Judy.

" Just you bring him indoors at once," said Mrs. Bird. " Why, he might catch his death of cold. I've a good mind to send him to bed without any supper."

It wasn't that Mrs. Bird was cross with Paddington— she was simply worried in case anything happened to him, and when he came through the door her manner changed at once.

She took one of his paws in her hand and then felt his nose. "Good gracious!" she exclaimed. "He's like an iceberg."

Paddington shivered. "I don't think I like being a snowbear very much," he said, in a weak voice.

"I should think not indeed," exclaimed Mrs. Bird. She turned to the others. "That bear's going to bed at once—with a hot-water bottle and a bowl of broth. Then I'm sending for the doctor."

With that she made Paddington sit by the fire while she hurried upstairs to fetch a thermometer.

Paddington lay back in Mr. Brown's armchair with his eyes closed. He certainly felt very strange. He couldn't remember ever having felt like it before. One moment he seemed to be as cold as the snow outside, the next he felt as if he was on fire.

He wasn't quite sure how long he lay there, but he vaguely remembered Mrs. Bird sticking something long and cold under his tongue, which she told him not to bite. After that he didn't remember much more, except that everyone started running around, preparing soup and filling hot-water bottles, and generally making sure his room was comfortable for him.

Within a few minutes everything was ready and the Browns all trooped upstairs to make sure he was properly tucked in bed. Paddington thanked them all very much and then, after waving a paw limply in their direction, lay back and closed his eyes.

" He *must* be feeling bad," whispered Mrs. Bird. " He hasn't even touched his soup."

" Gosh," said Jonathan, miserably, as he followed Judy down the stairs. " It was mostly my idea. I shall never forgive myself if anything happens to him."

" It was my idea as well," said Judy, comfortingly. " I expect we all thought of it together. Anyway," she added, as the front door bell rang, " that must be the doctor—so we shall soon know."

Doctor MacAndrew was a long time with Paddington, and when he came downstairs again he looked very serious.

" How is he, Doctor?" asked Mrs. Brown, anxiously. " He's not seriously ill, is he?"

" Aye, he is," said Doctor MacAndrew. " Ye may as well know. That young bear's verra ill indeed. Playing in the snow when he's not used to it no doubt. I've given him a wee drop o' medicine to tide him over the night and I'll be along first thing in the morning."

" But he *is* going to be all right, isn't he, Doctor MacAndrew?" cried Judy.

Doctor MacAndrew shook his head gravely. " I wouldna care to give an opinion," he said. " I wouldna care to give an opinion at all." With that he bade them all good-night and drove away.

It was a very sad party of Browns that went upstairs

that evening. While they were getting ready for bed, Mrs. Bird quietly moved her things into Paddington's room so that she could keep an eye on him during the night.

But she wasn't the only one who couldn't think of sleep. Several times the door to Paddington's room gently opened and either Mr. and Mrs. Brown or Jonathan and Judy crept in to see how he was getting on. Somehow it didn't seem possible that anything *could* happen to Paddington. But every time they looked at Mrs. Bird she just shook her head and went on with her sewing so that they couldn't see her face.

The next day the news of Paddington's illness quickly spread around the neighbourhood and by lunch time there was a steady stream of callers asking after him.

Mr. Gruber was the first on the scene. " I wondered what had happened to young Mr. Brown when he didn't turn up for elevenses this morning," he said, looking very upset. " I kept his cocoa hot for over an hour."

Mr. Gruber went away again, but returned shortly afterwards carrying a bunch of grapes and a large basket of fruit and flowers from the rest of the traders in the Portobello market. " I'm afraid there isn't much about at this time of the year," he said apologetically. " But we've done the best we can."

He paused at the door. " I'm sure he'll be all right, Mrs. Brown," he said. " With so many people *wanting* him to get well, I'm sure he will."

Mr. Gruber raised his hat to Mrs. Brown and then began walking slowly in the direction of the park. Somehow he didn't want to go back to his shop that day.

Even Mr. Curry knocked on the door that afternoon and brought with him an apple and a jar of calves' foot jelly, which he said was very good for invalids.

Mrs. Bird took all the presents up to Paddington's room and placed them carefully beside his bed in case he should wake up and want something to eat.

Doctor MacAndrew called a number of times during the next two days, but despite everything he did, there seemed to be no change at all. " We'll just have to bide our time," was all he would say.

It was three days later, at breakfast time, that the door to the Browns' dining-room burst open and Mrs. Bird rushed in.

" Oh, do come quickly," she cried. " It's Paddington! "

Everyone jumped up from the table and stared at Mrs. Bird.

" He's . . . he's not worse, is he? " asked Mrs. Brown, voicing the thoughts of them all.

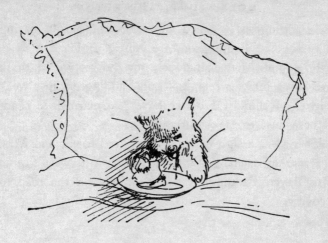

"Mercy me, no," said Mrs. Bird, fanning herself with the morning paper. "That's what I'm trying to tell you. He's much better. He's sitting up in bed asking for a marmalade sandwich!"

"A marmalade sandwich?" exclaimed Mrs. Brown. "Oh, thank goodness!" She wasn't quite sure whether she wanted to laugh or cry. "I never knew hearing the word marmalade could make me feel so happy."

Just as she spoke there was a loud ring from the bell which Mr. Brown had installed by the side of Paddington's bed in case of emergency.

"Oh dear," exclaimed Mrs. Bird. "I hope I haven't spoken too soon!" She rushed out of the room and everyone followed her up the stairs to Paddington's room. When they entered, Paddington was lying on his back with his paws in the air, staring up at the ceiling.

"Paddington!" called Mrs. Brown, hardly daring to breathe. "Paddington, are you all right?"

Everyone listened anxiously for the reply. "I think I've had a bit of a relapse," said Paddington, in a weak voice. "I think I'd better have *two* marmalade sandwiches—just to make sure."

There was a sigh of relief from the Browns and Mrs. Bird as they exchanged glances. Even if he wasn't quite himself yet, Paddington was definitely on the road to recovery.

CHAPTER SIX

Paddington and the Christmas Shopping

"I suppose I shouldn't say it," remarked Mrs. Bird, "but I shall be glad when Christmas is over."

The few weeks before Christmas were usually busy ones for Mrs. Bird. There were so many mince-pies, puddings and cakes to be made that much of her time was spent in the kitchen. This year matters hadn't been helped by the fact that Paddington was at home for most of the day "convalescing" after his illness. Paddington was very interested in mince-pies, and if he had opened the oven door once to see how they were getting on, he'd done it a dozen times.

Paddington's convalescence had been a difficult time for the Browns. While he had remained in bed it had been bad enough, because he kept getting grape-pips all over the sheets. But if anything, matters had got worse once he was up and about. He wasn't very good at "doing nothing" and it had become a full time occupation keeping him amused and out of trouble. He had even had several goes at knitting something—no one ever quite knew what—but he'd got in such a tangle with the wool, and it had become so sticky with marmalade, that in the end they had to throw it away. Even the dustman had said some very nasty things about it when he came to collect the rubbish.

"He seems very quiet at the moment," said Mrs. Brown. "I think he's busy with his Christmas list."

"You're not *really* taking him shopping with you this afternoon, are you?" asked Mrs. Bird. "You know what happened last time."*

Mrs. Brown sighed. She had vivid memories of the last time she had taken Paddington shopping. "I can't *not* take him," she said. "I did promise and he's been looking forward to it so much."

Paddington liked shopping. He always enjoyed looking in the shop windows and since he had read in the paper about all the Christmas decorations, he had thought of very little else. Besides, he had a special

* See *A Bear Called Paddington*

reason for wanting to go shopping this time. Although he hadn't told anyone, Paddington had been saving hard for some while in order to buy the Browns and his other friends some presents.

He had already bought a frame for his picture and sent it, together with a large jar of honey, to his Aunt Lucy in Peru, because presents for overseas had to be posted early.

He had several lists marked "SEACRET" which were locked away in his case, and he had been keeping his ears open for some time listening to conversation in the hope of finding something they all needed.

"Anyway," said Mrs. Brown, "it's so nice having him around again, and he's been so good lately, I think he ought to have a treat."

"Besides," she added, "I'm not taking him to Barkridges this time—I'm taking him to Crumbold and Ferns."

Mrs. Bird put down her baking tray. "Are you sure you're doing the right thing taking him there?" she exclaimed. "You know what they're like."

Crumbold and Ferns was a very old established shop where everyone spoke in whispers and all the assistants wore frock-coats. Only the best people went to Crumbold and Ferns.

"It's Christmas," said Mrs. Brown, recklessly. "It'll be a nice treat for him."

And when Paddington set off with Mrs. Brown after lunch, even Mrs. Bird had to admit he looked smart enough to go anywhere. His duffle coat, which had just come back from the cleaners, was spotlessly clean, and even his old hat—which Paddington always insisted on wearing when he went on shopping expeditions—looked unusually neat.

All the same, as Paddington waved his paw at the corner, and Mrs. Bird turned to go back indoors, she couldn't help feeling glad she was staying at home.

Paddington enjoyed the journey to Crumbold and Ferns. They went by bus and he managed to get a front seat downstairs. By standing on the seat he could just see through the little hole in the screen behind the driver's back. Paddington tapped on the glass several times and waved his paw at the man behind the wheel, but he was much too busy with the traffic to look round—in fact they drove a long way without stopping at all.

The conductor was cross when he saw what Paddington was doing. " Oi! " he shouted. " Stop that there tapping! It's bears like you what get buses a bad name. We've gone past three queues already."

But he was a kindly man and when Paddington said he was sorry, he explained to him all about the signals for making buses stop or go on, and he gave him the end of a roll of tickets as a present. When he had collected all the fares, he came back again and pointed out some buildings of interest to Paddington as they passed them. He even presented him with a large bullseye which he found in his money bag. Paddington liked seeing new places and he was sorry when the journey came to an end and he had to say good-bye to the conductor.

There was another slight upset when they reached Crumbold and Ferns. Paddington had an accident with the revolving door. It wasn't really his fault, but he tried to follow Mrs. Brown into the store just as a very distinguished-looking gentleman with a beard came out the other side. The man was in a great hurry and when he pushed the revolving door it started going round at great speed, taking Paddington with it. He went round several times until he found to his astonishment that he was outside on the pavement once more.

He had a brief glimpse of the man with the beard waving to him from the back of a large car as it drove away. The man also appeared to be shouting something, but Paddington never knew what it was, for at that moment he trod on something sharp and fell over backwards again.

He sat in the middle of the pavement examining his foot and found to his surprise that it had a tie-pin sticking in it. Paddington knew it was a tie-pin because Mr. Brown had one very like it—except that his was quite ordinary, whereas this one had something big and shiny fixed to the middle of it. Paddington pinned it to the front of his duffle coat for safety and then suddenly became aware that someone was speaking to him.

" Are you all right, sir? " It was the doorkeeper— a very dignified man in a smart uniform with lots of medals.

" I think so, thank you," said Paddington, as he stood up and dusted himself, " but I've lost my bullseye somewhere."

" Your bullseye? " said the man. " Dear me! " If he felt surprised he showed no signs of it. Doorkeepers at Crumbold and Ferns were always very well trained. All the same, he couldn't help wondering about Paddington. When he noticed the tie-pin with the enormous diamond in the middle, he realised at once that he was dealing with someone very important. " Probably one of these society bears," he thought to himself. But when he caught sight of Paddington's old hat he wasn't quite so sure. " Perhaps he's a huntin', shootin' and fishin' bear up from the country for the day," he decided. " Or even a society bear that's seen better days."

So he held up the passers-by with a stern wave of the hand while they searched the pavement. As he guided Paddington back through the revolving door to Mrs. Brown, who was waiting anxiously on the other side, he tried hard to look as if helping a young bear of quality find his bullseye was an everyday event at Crumbold and Ferns.

Paddington returned his salute with a wave of the paw and then looked around. The inside of the shop was most impressive. Everywhere they went, tall men in frock-coats bowed low and wished them good afternoon. Paddington's paw was quite tired by the time they reached the Household department.

As they both had some secret shopping to do, Mrs.

Brown left Paddington with the assistant and arranged to meet him outside the entrance to the shop in a quarter of an hour.

The man assured Mrs. Brown that Paddington would be quite safe. "Although I don't recall any actual bears," he said, when she explained that Paddington came from Darkest Peru, "we have a number of very distinguished foreign gentlemen among our clients. Many of them do all their Christmas shopping here."

He turned and looked down at Paddington as Mrs. Brown left, brushing an imaginary speck of dust from his frock-coat.

Secretly Paddington was feeling rather overawed by Crumbold and Ferns, and not wishing to disgrace Mrs. Brown by doing the wrong thing, he gave his own coat a passing tap with his paw. The assistant watched with fascination as a small cloud of dust rose into the air and then slowly settled on his nice, clean counter.

Paddington followed the man's gaze. "I expect it came off the pavement," he said, by way of explanation. "I had an accident in the revolving door."

The man coughed. "Oh dear," he said. "How very unfortunate." He gave Paddington a sickly smile and decided to ignore the whole matter. "And what can we do for you, sir?" he asked, brightly.

Paddington looked round carefully to make sure Mrs. Brown was nowhere in sight. "I want a clothes line," he announced.

"A *what?*" exclaimed the assistant.

Paddington hurriedly moved the bullseye to the other side of his mouth. " A clothes line," he repeated, in a muffled voice. " It's for Mrs. Bird. Her old one broke the other day."

The assistant swallowed hard. He found it impossible to understand what this extraordinary young bear was saying.

" Perhaps," he suggested, for a Crumbold and Ferns assistant rarely bent down, " you wouldn't mind standing on the counter? "

Paddington sighed. It really was most difficult trying to explain things sometimes. Climbing up on to the counter he unlocked his suitcase and withdrew an advertisement which he'd cut from Mr. Brown's newspaper several days before.

" Ah! " The assistant's face cleared. " You mean one of our special *expanding* clothes lines, sir." He reached up to a shelf and picked out a small green box. " A very suitable choice, if I may say so, sir. As befits a young bear of taste. I can thoroughly recommend it."

The man pulled a piece of rope through a hole in the side of the box and handed it to Paddington. " This type of expanding clothes line is used by some of the best families in the country."

Paddington looked suitably impressed as he climbed down, holding on to the rope with his paw.

" You see," continued the man, bending over the counter, " it is all quite simple. The clothes line is all contained inside this box. As you walk away with the rope, it unwinds itself. Then, when you have finished with it, you simply turn this handle and . . ." A puzzled note came into his voice.

"You simply turn this handle," he repeated, trying again. Really, it was all most annoying. Instead of the clothes line going back into the box as it was supposed to, more was actually coming out.

"I'm extremely sorry, sir," he began, looking up from the counter. "Something seems to have jammed. . . ." His voice trailed away and a worried look came into his eyes, for Paddington was nowhere in sight.

"I say," he called, to another assistant farther along the counter. "Have you seen a young bear gentleman go past—pulling on a clothes line?"

"He went that way," replied the other man, briefly. He pointed towards the china department. "I think he got caught in the crowd."

"Oh dear," said Paddington's assistant, as he picked up the green box and began pushing his way through the crowd of shoppers, following the trail of the clothes line. "Oh dear! Oh dear!"

As it happened, the assistant wasn't the only one to feel worried. At the other end of the clothes line Paddington was already in trouble. Crumbold and Ferns was filled with people doing their Christmas shopping, and none of them seemed to have time for a small bear. Several times he'd had to crawl under a table in order to avoid being trodden on.

It was a very good clothes line, and Paddington felt
sure Mrs. Bird would like it. But he couldn't help
wishing he'd chosen something else. There seemed to
be no end to it, and he kept getting it tangled round
people's legs.

He went on and on, round a table laden with cups and
saucers, past a pillar, underneath another table, and still
the clothes line trailed after him. All the time the crowd
was getting thicker and thicker and Paddington had to
push hard to make any headway at all. Once or twice he
nearly lost his hat.

Just as he had almost given up hope of ever finding
his way back to the Household department again, he
caught sight of the assistant. To Paddington's surprise,

the man was sitting on the floor, looking very red in the face. His hair was all ruffled and he appeared to be struggling with a table leg.

"Ah, there you are!" he gasped, when he caught sight of Paddington. "I suppose you realise, young bear, I've been following you all round the china department. Now you've tied everything up in knots."

"Oh dear," said Paddington, looking at the rope.

" Did *I* do that? I'm afraid I got lost. Bears aren't very good in crowds, you know. I must have gone under the same table twice."

" What have you done with the other end? " shouted the assistant.

He wasn't in the best of tempers. It was hot and noisy under the table and people kept kicking him. Apart from that, it was most undignified.

" It's here," said Paddington, trying to find his end of the rope. " At least—it was a moment ago."

" Where? " shouted the assistant. He didn't know whether it was simply the noise of the crowd, but he still couldn't understand a word this young bear uttered. Whenever he did say anything it seemed to be accompanied by a strange crunching noise and a strong smell of peppermint.

" Speak up," he shouted, cupping a hand to his ear. " I can't hear a word you say."

Paddington looked at the man uneasily. He looked rather cross and he was beginning to wish he had left his bullseye on the pavement outside. It was a very nice bullseye but it made talking most difficult.

It was as he felt in his duffle coat pocket for a hand-kerchief that it happened.

The assistant jumped slightly and the expression on his face froze and then gradually changed to one of disbelief.

" Excuse me," said Paddington, tapping him on the

shoulder, " but I think my bullseye has fallen in your ear!"

"Your *bullseye*?" exclaimed the man, in a horrified tone of voice. "Fallen in my ear?"

"Yes," said Paddington. "It was given to me by a bus conductor and I'm afraid it's got a bit slippery where I've been sucking it."

The assistant crawled out from under the table and drew himself up to his full height. With a look of great distaste, he withdrew the remains of Paddington's bullseye from his ear. He held it for a moment between thumb and forefinger and then hurriedly placed it on a nearby counter. It was bad enough having to crawl around the floor untangling a clothes line—but to have a bullseye in his ear—such a thing had never been known before in Crumbold and Ferns.

He took a deep breath and pointed a trembling finger in Paddington's direction. But as he opened his mouth to speak he noticed that Paddington was no longer there. Neither, for that matter, was the clothes line. He was only just in time to grab the table as it rocked on its legs. As it was, several plates and a cup and saucer fell to the floor.

The assistant raised his eyes to the ceiling and made a mental note to avoid any young bears who came into the shop in future.

There seemed to be a commotion going on in the direction of the entrance hall. He had his own ideas on the possible cause of it, but wisely he decided to keep his thoughts to himself. He had had quite enough to do with bear customers for one day.

Mrs. Brown pushed her way through the crowd which had formed on the pavement outside Crumbold and Ferns.

"Excuse me," she said, pulling on the doorkeeper's sleeve. "Excuse me. You haven't seen a young bear in a blue duffle coat, have you? We arranged to meet here and there are so many people about I'm really rather worried."

The doorkeeper touched his cap. "That wouldn't be the young gentleman in question, ma'am?" he asked, pointing through a gap in the crowd to where another man in uniform was struggling with the revolving door. "If it is—he's stuck! Good and proper. Can't get in and can't get out. Right in the middle he is, so to speak."

"Oh dear," said Mrs. Brown. "That certainly sounds as if it might be Paddington."

Standing on tip-toe, she peered over the shoulder of a bearded gentleman in front of her. The man was shouting words of encouragement as he tapped on the glass and she just caught a glimpse of a familiar paw as it waved back in acknowledgment.

"It *is* Paddington," she exclaimed. "Now how on earth did he get in there?"

"Ah," said the doorkeeper. "That's just what we're trying to find out. Something to do with 'is getting a clothes line wrapped round the 'inges, so they say."

There was a ripple of excitement from the crowd as the door started to revolve once more.

Everyone made a rush for Paddington, but the distinguished man with the beard reached him first. To everyone's surprise, he took hold of his paw and began pumping it up and down.

" Thank you, bear," he kept saying. " Glad to know you, bear ! "

" Glad to know *you*," repeated Paddington, looking as surprised as anyone.

" I say," exclaimed the doorkeeper respectfully, as he turned to Mrs. Brown. " I didn't know he was a friend of Sir Gresholm Gibbs."

" Neither did I," said Mrs. Brown. " And who might Sir Gresholm Gibbs be ? "

" Sir Gresholm," repeated the doorkeeper, in a hushed voice. " Why, he's a famous millionaire. He's one of Crumbold and Ferns' most important customers."

He pushed back the crowd of interested spectators to allow Paddington and the distinguished man a free passage.

" Dear lady," said Sir Gresholm, bowing low as he approached. " You must be Mrs. Brown. I've just been hearing all about you."

" Oh ? " said Mrs. Brown, doubtfully.

" This young bear of yours found a most valuable diamond tie-pin which I lost earlier this afternoon," said Sir Gresholm. " Not only that, but he's kept it in safe custody all this time."

"A diamond tie-pin?" exclaimed Mrs. Brown, looking at Paddington. It was the first she had heard of any diamond tie-pin.

"I found it when I lost my bullseye," said Paddington, in a loud stage whisper.

"An example to us all," boomed Sir Gresholm, as he turned to the crowd and pointed at Paddington.

Paddington waved a paw modestly in the air as one or two people applauded.

"And now, dear lady," continued Sir Gresholm, turning to Mrs. Brown. "I understand you intend showing this young bear some of the Christmas decorations."

"Well," said Mrs. Brown. "I was hoping to. He hasn't seen them before and it's really his first trip out since he was ill."

"In that case," said Sir Gresholm, waving to a luxurious car which was parked by the side of the pavement. "my car is at your disposal."

"Ooh," said Paddington. "Is it really?" His eyes glistened. He'd never seen such an enormous car before, let alone ever dreamt of riding in one.

"Yes, indeed," said Sir Gresholm, as he held the door open for them. "That is," he added, as he noticed a worried expression cross Paddington's face, "if you would do me the honour."

"Oh, yes," said Paddington, politely. "I would like to do you the honour very much indeed." He hesitated. "But I've left my bullseye on one of the counters in Crumbold and Ferns."

"Oh dear," said the gentleman, as he helped Paddington and Mrs. Brown into the car. "Then there's only one thing we can do."

He tapped on the glass window behind the driver

with his stick. "Drive on, James," he said. "And don't stop until we reach the nearest sweet shop."

"One with bullseyes, please, Mr. James," called Paddington.

"Definitely one with bullseyes," repeated Sir Gresholm. "That's most important." He turned to Mrs. Brown with a twinkle in his eye. "You know," he said, "I'm looking forward to this."

" So am I," said Paddington earnestly, as he gazed out of the window at all the lights.

As the huge car drew away from the kerb he stood on the seat and gave a final wave of his paw to the crowd of open-mouthed spectators, and then settled back, holding on to a long gold tassel with his other paw.

It wasn't every day a bear was able to ride round London in such a magnificent car and Paddington wanted to enjoy it to the full.

CHAPTER SEVEN

Christmas

PADDINGTON FOUND that Christmas took a long time to come. Each morning when he hurried downstairs he crossed the date off the calendar, but the more days he crossed off the farther away it seemed.

However, there was plenty to occupy his mind. For one thing, the postman started arriving later and later in the morning, and when he did finally reach the Browns' house there were so many letters to deliver he had a job to push them all through the letter-box. Often there were mysterious-looking parcels as well, which Mrs. Bird promptly hid before Paddington had time to squeeze them.

A surprising number of the envelopes were addressed to Paddington himself, and he carefully made a list of all those who had sent him Christmas cards so that he could be sure of thanking them.

" You may be only a small bear," said Mrs. Bird, as she helped him arrange the cards on the mantelpiece, " but you certainly leave your mark."

Paddington wasn't sure how to take this, especially as Mrs. Bird had just polished the hall floor, but when he examined his paws they were quite clean.

Paddington had made his own Christmas cards. Some he had drawn himself, decorating the edges with holly and mistletoe; others had been made out of pictures cut from Mrs. Brown's magazines. But each one had the words A MERRY CHRISTMAS AND A HAPPY NEW YEAR printed on the front, and they were signed PADINGTUN BROWN on the inside—together with his special paw mark to show that they were genuine.

Paddington wasn't sure about the spelling of A MERRY CHRISTMAS. It didn't look at all right. But Mrs. Bird checked all the words in a dictionary for him to make certain.

" I don't suppose many people get Christmas cards from a bear," she explained. " They'll probably want to keep them, so you ought to make sure they are right."

One evening Mr. Brown arrived home with a huge Christmas tree tied to the roof of his car. It was placed in a position of honour by the dining-room window and both Paddington and Mr. Brown spent a long time decorating it with coloured electric lights and silver tinsel.

Apart from the Christmas tree, there were paper chains and holly to be put up, and large coloured bells made of crinkly paper. Paddington enjoyed doing the paper chains. He managed to persuade Mr. Brown that bears were very good at putting up decorations and together they did most of the house, with Paddington standing on Mr. Brown's shoulders while Mr. Brown handed up the drawing pins. It came to an unhappy end one evening when Paddington accidentally put his paw on a drawing pin which he'd left on top of Mr. Brown's head. When Mrs. Bird rushed into the dining-room to see what all the fuss was about, and to inquire why all the lights had suddenly gone out, she found Paddington hanging by his paws from the chandelier and Mr. Brown dancing round the room rubbing his head.

But by then the decorations were almost finished and the house had taken on quite a festive air. The sideboard was groaning under the weight of nuts and oranges, dates and figs, none of which Paddington was allowed to touch, and Mr. Brown had stopped smoking his pipe and was filling the air instead with the smell of cigars.

The excitement in the Browns' house mounted, until it reached fever pitch a few days before Christmas, when Jonathan and Judy arrived home for the holidays.

But if the days leading up to Christmas were busy and

exciting, they were nothing compared with Christmas day itself.

The Browns were up early on Christmas morning—much earlier than they had intended. It all started when Paddington woke to find a large pillow case at the bottom of his bed. His eyes nearly popped out with astonishment when he switched his torch on, for it was bulging with parcels, and it certainly hadn't been there when he'd gone to bed on Christmas Eve.

Paddington's eyes grew larger and larger as he unwrapped the brightly coloured paper round each present. A few days before, on Mrs. Bird's instructions, he had made a list of all the things he hoped to have given him and had hidden it up one of the chimneys. It was a strange thing, but everything on that list seemed to be in the pillow case.

There was a large chemistry outfit from Mr. Brown, full of jars and bottles and test tubes, which looked very interesting. And there was a miniature xylophone from Mrs. Brown, which pleased him no end. Paddington was fond of music—especially the loud sort, which was good for conducting—and he had always wanted something he could actually play.

Mrs. Bird's parcel was even more exciting, for it contained a checked cap which he'd especially asked for and had underlined on his list. Paddington stood on the end of his bed, admiring the effect in the mirror for quite a while.

Jonathan and Judy had each given him a travel book. Paddington was very interested in geography, being a much-travelled bear, and he was pleased to see there were plenty of maps and coloured pictures inside.

The noise from Paddington's room was soon sufficient to waken both Jonathan and Judy, and in no time at all the whole house was in an uproar, with wrapping paper and bits of string everywhere.

" I'm as patriotic as the next man," grumbled Mr. Brown. " But I draw the line when bears start playing the National Anthem at six o'clock in the morning—especially on a xylophone."

As always, it was left to Mrs. Bird to restore order. " No more presents until after lunch," she said, firmly. She had just tripped over Paddington on the upstairs landing, where he was investigating his new chemical outfit, and something nasty had gone in one of her slippers.

" It's all right, Mrs. Bird," said Paddington, consulting his instruction book, " it's only some iron filings. I don't think they're dangerous."

" Dangerous or not," said Mrs. Bird, " I've a big dinner to cook—not to mention your birthday cake to finish decorating."

Being a bear, Paddington had two birthdays each year—one in the summer and one at Christmas—and the Browns were holding a party in his honour to which Mr. Gruber had been invited.

After they'd had breakfast and been to church, the

morning passed quickly and Paddington spent most of his time trying to decide what to do next. With so many things from which to choose it was most difficult. He read some chapters from his books and made several interesting smells and a small explosion with his chemical outfit.

Mr. Brown was already in trouble for having given it to him, especially when Paddington found a chapter in the instruction book headed " Indoor Fireworks." He made himself a " never ending " snake which wouldn't stop growing and frightened Mrs. Bird to death when she met it coming down the stairs.

" If we don't watch out," she confided to Mrs. Brown, " we shan't last over Christmas. We shall either be blown to smithereens or poisoned. He was testing my gravy with some litmus paper just now."

Mrs. Brown sighed. " It's a good job Christmas only comes once a year," she said, as she helped Mrs. Bird with the potatoes.

" It isn't over yet," warned Mrs. Bird.

Fortunately, Mr. Gruber arrived at that moment and some measure of order was established before they all sat down to dinner.

Paddington's eyes glistened as he surveyed the table. He didn't agree with Mr. Brown when he said it all looked too good to eat. All the same, even Paddington got noticeably slower towards the end when Mrs. Bird brought in the Christmas pudding.

" Well," said Mr. Gruber, a few minutes later, as he

sat back and surveyed his empty plate, " I must say that's the best Christmas dinner I've had for many a day. Thank you very much indeed! "

" Hear! Hear! " agreed Mr. Brown. " What do you say, Paddington? "

" It was very nice," said Paddington, licking some cream from his whiskers. " Except I had a bone in my Christmas pudding."

" You *what*? " exclaimed Mrs. Brown. " Don't be silly—there are no bones in Christmas pudding."

" I had one," said Paddington, firmly. " It was all hard—and it stuck in my throat."

" Good gracious! " exclaimed Mrs. Bird. " The sixpence! I always put a piece of silver in the Christmas pudding."

" What! " said Paddington, nearly falling off his chair. " A sixpence? I've never heard of a sixpence pudding before."

" Quick," shouted Mr. Brown, rising to the emergency. " Turn him upside down."

Before Paddington could reply, he found himself hanging head downwards while Mr. Brown and Mr. Gruber took it in turns to shake him. The rest of the family stood round watching the floor.

" It's no good," said Mr. Brown, after a while. " It must have gone too far." He helped Mr. Gruber lift Paddington into an armchair where he lay gasping for breath.

" I've got a magnet upstairs," said Jonathan. " We

could try lowering it down his throat on a piece of string."

" I don't think so, dear," said Mrs. Brown, in a worried tone of voice. " He might swallow that and then we should be even worse off." She bent over the chair. " How do you feel, Paddington? "

" Sick," said Paddington, in an aggrieved tone of voice.

" Of course you do, dear," said Mrs. Brown. " It's only to be expected. There's only one thing to do— we shall have to send for the doctor."

" Thank goodness I scrubbed it first," said Mrs. Bird. " It might have been covered with germs."

" But I *didn't* swallow it," gasped Paddington. " I only nearly did. Then I put it on the side of my plate. I didn't know it was a sixpence because it was all covered with Christmas pudding."

Paddington felt very fed up. He'd just eaten one of the best dinners he could ever remember and now he'd been turned upside down and shaken without even being given time to explain.

Everyone exchanged glances and then crept quietly away, leaving Paddington to recover by himself. There didn't seem to be much they *could* say.

But after the dinner things had been cleared away, and by the time Mrs. Bird had made some strong coffee, Paddington was almost himself again. He was sitting up in the chair helping himself to some dates when they trooped back into the room. It took a lot to make Paddington ill for very long.

When they had finished their coffee, and were sitting round the blazing fire feeling warm and comfortable, Mr. Brown rubbed his hands. " Now, Paddington," he said, " it's not only Christmas, it's your birthday as well. What would you like to do? "

A mysterious expression came over Paddington's face. " If you all go in the other room," he announced, " I've a special surprise for you."

" Oh dear, *must* we, Paddington? " said Mrs. Brown. " There isn't a fire."

" I shan't be long," said Paddington, firmly. " But it's a special surprise and it has to be prepared." He held the door open and the Browns, Mrs. Bird and Mr. Gruber filed obediently into the other room.

" Now close your eyes," said Paddington, when they were all settled, " and I'll let you know when I'm ready."

Mrs. Brown shivered. " I hope you won't be too long," she called. But the only reply was the sound of the door clicking shut.

They waited for several minutes without speaking, and then Mr. Gruber cleared his throat. " Do you think young Mr. Brown's forgotten about us? " he asked.

" I don't know," said Mrs. Brown. " But I'm not waiting much longer."

" Henry! " she exclaimed, as she opened her eyes. " Have you gone to sleep? "

" Er, wassat? " snorted Mr. Brown. He had eaten such a large dinner he was finding it difficult to keep awake. " What's happening? Have I missed anything? "

" Nothing's happening," said Mrs. Brown. " Henry, you'd better go and see what Paddington's up to."

Several more minutes went by before Mr. Brown returned to announce that he couldn't find Paddington anywhere.

" Well, he must be *somewhere*," said Mrs. Brown. " Bears don't disappear into thin air."

" Crikey! " exclaimed Jonathan, as a thought suddenly struck him. " You don't think he's playing at Father Christmas, do you? He was asking all about it the other day when he put his list up the chimney. I bet that's why he wanted us to come in here—because this chimney connects with the one upstairs—and there isn't a fire."

" Father Christmas? " said Mr. Brown. " I'll give him Father Christmas! " He stuck his head up the chimney and called Paddington's name several times. " I can't see anything," he said, striking a match. As if in answer a large lump of soot descended and burst on top of his head.

" Now look what you've done, Henry," said Mrs. Brown. " Shouting so—you've disturbed the soot. All over your clean shirt!"

" If it *is* young Mr. Brown, perhaps he's stuck somewhere," suggested Mr. Gruber. " He did have rather a large dinner. I remember wondering at the time where he put it all."

Mr. Gruber's suggestion had an immediate effect on the party and everyone began to look serious.

" Why, he might suffocate with the fumes," exclaimed Mrs. Bird, as she hurried outside to the broom cupboard.

When she returned, armed with a mop, everyone took it in turns to poke it up the chimney but even though they strained their ears they couldn't hear a sound.

It was while the excitement was at its height that Paddington came into the room. He looked most surprised when he saw Mr. Brown with his head up the chimney.

" You can come into the dining-room now," he announced, looking round the room. " I've finished wrapping my presents and they're all on the Christmas tree."

" You don't mean to say," spluttered Mr. Brown, as he sat in the fireplace rubbing his face with a handkerchief, " you've been in the other room all the time? "

" Yes," said Paddington, innocently. " I hope I didn't keep you waiting too long."

Mrs. Brown looked at her husband. " I thought you said you'd looked everywhere," she exclaimed.

" Well—we'd just come from the dining-room," said Mr. Brown, looking very sheepish. " I didn't think he'd be *there*."

" It only goes to show," said Mrs. Bird hastily, as she caught sight of the expression on Mr. Brown's face, " how easy it is to give a bear a bad name."

Paddington looked most interested when they explained to him what all the fuss was about.

" I never thought of coming down the chimney," he said, staring at the fireplace.

" Well, you're not thinking about it now either," replied Mr. Brown, sternly.

But even Mr. Brown's expression changed as he

followed Paddington into the dining-room and saw the surprise that had been prepared for them.

In addition to the presents that had already been placed on the tree, there were now six newly wrapped ones tied to the lower branches. If the Browns recognised the wrapping paper they had used for Paddington's presents earlier in the day, they were much too polite to say anything.

" I'm afraid I had to use old paper," said Paddington apologetically, as he waved a paw at the tree. " I hadn't any money left. That's why you had to go in the other room while I wrapped them."

" Really, Paddington," said Mrs. Brown. " I'm very cross with you—spending all your money on presents for us."

" I'm afraid they're rather ordinary," said Paddington, as he settled back in a chair to watch the others. " But I hope you like them. They're all labelled so that you know which is which."

" Ordinary? " exclaimed Mr. Brown, as he opened his parcel. " I don't call a pipe rack ordinary. And there's an ounce of my favourite tobacco tied to the back as well! "

" Gosh! A new stamp album! " cried Jonathan. " Whizzo! And it's got some stamps inside already."

" They're Peruvian ones from Aunt Lucy's postcards," said Paddington. " I've been saving them for you."

" And I've got a box of paints," exclaimed Judy.

" Thank you very much, Paddington. It's just what I wanted."

" We all seem to be lucky," said Mrs. Brown, as she unwrapped a parcel containing a bottle of her favourite lavender water. " How *did* you guess? I finished my last bottle only a week ago."

" I'm sorry about your parcel, Mrs. Bird," said Paddington, looking across the room. " I had a bit of a job with the knots."

" It must be something special," said Mr. Brown. " It seems all string and no parcel."

" That's because it's really clothes line," explained Paddington, " not string. I rescued it when I got stuck in the revolving door at Crumbold and Ferns."

" That makes two presents in one," said Mrs. Bird, as she freed the last of the knots and began unwinding yards and yards of paper. " How exciting. I can't think what it can be."

" Why," she exclaimed. " I do believe it's a brooch! And it's shaped like a bear—how lovely! " Mrs. Bird looked most touched as she handed the present round for everyone to see. " I shall keep it in a safe place," she added, " and only wear it on special occasions— when I want to impress people."

" I don't know what mine is," said Mr. Gruber, as they all turned to him. He squeezed the parcel. " It's such a funny shape."

" It's a drinking mug! " he exclaimed, his face

lighting up with pleasure. "And it even has my name painted on the side!"

"It's for your elevenses, Mr. Gruber," said Paddington. "I noticed your old one was getting rather chipped."

"I'm sure it will make my cocoa taste better than it ever has before," said Mr. Gruber.

He stood up and cleared his throat. "I think I would like to offer a vote of thanks to young Mr. Brown," he said, "for all his nice presents. I'm sure he must have given them a great deal of thought."

"Hear! Hear!" echoed Mr. Brown, as he filled his pipe.

Mr. Gruber felt under his chair. "And while I think of it, Mr. Brown, I have a small present for you."

Everyone stood round and watched while Paddington struggled with his parcel, eager to see what Mr. Gruber had bought him. A gasp of surprise went up as he tore the paper to one side, for it was a beautifully bound leather scrapbook, with "Paddington Brown" printed in gold leaf on the cover.

Paddington didn't know what to say, but Mr. Gruber waved his thanks to one side. "I know how you enjoy writing about your adventures, Mr. Brown," he said. "And you have so many I'm sure your present scrapbook must be almost full."

"It is," said Paddington, earnestly. "And I'm sure I shall have lots more. Things happen to me, you know. But I shall only put my best ones in here!"

When he made his way up to bed later that evening, his mind was in such a whirl, and he was so full of good things, he could hardly climb the stairs—let alone think about anything. He wasn't quite sure which he had enjoyed most. The presents, the Christmas dinner, the games, or the tea—with the special marmalade-layer birthday cake Mrs. Bird had made in his honour. Pausing on the corner half-way up, he decided he had enjoyed giving his own presents best of all.

"Paddington! Whatever have you got there?" He jumped and hastily hid his paw behind his back as he heard Mrs. Bird calling from the bottom of the stairs.

"It's only some sixpence pudding, Mrs. Bird," he called, looking over the banisters guiltily. "I thought I might get hungry during the night and I didn't want to take any chances."

"Honestly!" Mrs. Bird exclaimed, as she was joined by the others. "What *does* that bear look like? A paper hat about ten sizes too big on his head—Mr. Gruber's scrapbook in one paw—and a plate of Christmas pudding in the other!"

"I don't care what he looks like," said Mrs. Brown, "so long as he stays that way. The place wouldn't be the same without him."

But Paddington was too far away to hear what was being said. He was already sitting up in bed, busily writing in his scrapbook.

First of all, there was a very important notice to go on the front page. It said:

PADINGTUN BROWN,

32 WINDSOR GARDENS,

LUNDUN,

ENGLAND,

YUROPE,

THE WORLD.

Then, on the next page he added, in large capital letters: MY ADDVENTURES. CHAPTER WUN.

Paddington sucked his pen thoughtfully for a moment and then carefully replaced the top on the bottle of ink before it had a chance to fall over on the sheets. He felt much too sleepy to write any more. But he didn't really mind. To-morrow was another day—and he felt quite sure he *would* have some more adventures—even if he didn't know what they were going to be as yet.

Paddington lay back and pulled the blankets up round his whiskers. It was warm and comfortable and he sighed contentedly as he closed his eyes. It was nice being a bear. Especially a bear called Paddington.